Don't miss the first fin-flicking romance,
FORGIVE MY FINS

TERA LYNN CHILDS

FINS ARE FOREVER

KATHERINE TEGEN BOOKS
An Imprint of HarperCollins *Publishers*

Katherine Tegen Books is an imprint of HarperCollins Publishers.

Fins Are Forever
Copyright © 2011 by Tera Lynn Childs
All rights reserved.
Printed in the United States of America.
www.harperteen.com

Library of Congress Cataloging-in-Publication Data
Childs, Tera Lynn.
    Fins are forever / Tera Lynn Childs. — 1st ed.
        p.   cm.
    Summary: Half-mermaid half-human Princess Lily is about to renounce
her place in the royal succession of the undersea kingdom of Thalassinia, and
spend her life on land with the boy she loves, until her annoying cousin appears
and throws her decision into doubt.
    ISBN 978-0-06-191468-3 (trade bdg.)
    [1. Mermaids—Fiction.   2. Cousins—Fiction.   3. Interpersonal rela-
tions—Fiction.   4. High schools—Fiction.   5. Schools—Fiction.]   I. Title.
PZ7.C44185Fi 2011   2010023069
[Fic]—dc22   CIP
                                                                             AC

Typography by Andrea Vandergrift
11 12 13 14 15   LP/RRDB   10 9 8 7 6 5 4 3 2 1
❖
First Edition

For Jenny, because she keeps the crazy at bay

*A*t the moment I am sole heir to the throne of Thalassinia, one of the most prosperous underwater kingdoms in the world. I am a princess without equal in most of the seven seas, or any other body of water, for that matter. Raised to all the duties that my title requires and prepared to be my kingdom's future queen, I am respected, revered, and really, really loved by (most of) the people.

A mermaid and a princess, all wrapped into one. Talk about every little human girl's dream.

But come my eighteenth birthday in eighteen days—not that I'm counting—I'll be just a girl. Well, still a *mergirl*, true, but an *average* mergirl just the same.

At midnight, after my birthday ball, I will sign the renunciation paperwork, inking Princess Waterlily out of existence. In her place will be plain old Lily Sanderson, living on land, dating the boy she loves, and trying to figure out this human thing once and for all. I'm also facing a whole new wave of pressures that go along with the job—college, career, future, tests and applications and GPA and a million other little things that weren't even on my sonar when the plan was to return to Thalassinia after graduation next month.

It's a little overwhelming at times, which possibly explains why I'm doodling hearts and bubbles and L+Q=4EVA instead of copying Mr. Kingsley's notes from the board.

"There should be a law against having trig this late in the day," Quince complains from the desk next to mine.

Startled, I hastily cover my daydreamy notes with my textbook and look up at Quince. But his attention is focused—as mine should be—on our teacher and the equation on the board. I sigh with relief. I shouldn't be embarrassed by my love doodles, because we are officially a couple now, so I have every right. Still, I don't want him to think I'm any more of a lovesick guppy than he already knows.

Casually as I can, I flip to a clean page and try—pretend—to focus on math. My attention is still on Quince.

Head hanging down over my textbook, I slide another sideways glance at his handsome face. Mostly just because I can, but also because he's nice to look at. There's not much fault to find in his strong jaw, dark blond hair, and Caribbean blue eyes. Eyes that remind me of home.

Before the accidental kiss and bond that brought us together, he sat one row over, on the other side of my recently former crush, Brody. When I came back to Seaview and we started dating officially and for certain, Quince made Brody switch so he could sit next to me. I never knew Brody was such a pushover, but I'm glad. This is the only class Quince and I have together, and I'd rather have him at my side.

"I know, right," Brody says from one row over. "Maybe we should start an antitrig petition."

Quince laughs. He's been a lot nicer to Brody since I got over my ridiculous and unfounded crush and started dating *him* instead.

Tearing his attention away from the board, Quince turns to face me, catching me staring—okay, *ogling*. Even though, as his official girlfriend, I have free rein to stare—okay, *ogle*—I still can't stop the heat that blushes my cheeks to what I'm sure is an anemone shade of red.

"You're watching me, princess." His soft lips spread into an appreciative smile. "People might get the wrong idea."

"What, that I actually like you now?" I tease.

He shakes his head and leans toward me. "No, that you're trying to see past me to get an eyeful of Benson."

He tilts his head in Brody's direction. He knows it bugs me when he deliberately gets Brody's name wrong. But I'm learning not to rise to the bait. Instead, I fight back.

I shift my gaze to the board and fix an innocent look on my face.

"What makes you think that's the *wrong* idea?"

Quince leans even closer and says, "Because you came back for me."

"I—"

Thankfully I'm saved from coming up with a response by the bell signaling the end of sixth period. I'm getting better at trading barbs with him, but I'm not even close to his level yet.

Everyone, including Quince and me, hurriedly shoves their trig books into backpacks and messenger bags and bolts for the hall before Kingsley can assign the homework he's forgotten.

"I wish you had study hall," I say as we weave through the crowd. It would be nice if we had it together.

"Me, too," he says, placing a gentle hand on my lower back to guide me into an opening in the stream of students. "Between my job and your extracurriculars, I've barely gotten to see you since you came back."

"I know." I weave closer to him to avoid an overstuffed backpack. "It will be better after graduation."

"Then I'll start working full-time," he argues.

"It'll still be better," I insist. "No more homework until college."

If I get in, that is. My grades have been submediocre—partly because many of the subjects are completely foreign to the mer world, and partly because I never imagined going to college. I didn't need a degree to rule Thalassinia. Now that's all changed, and at my meeting with the school counselor this week, I learned that the only way I'll get into college—*any* college—is to ace the SATs. I've enlisted my genius best human friend's help and enrolled in an intensive test-prep class, but I'm not counting on a decent score. Tests and I don't really get along.

"You'll get in," Quince assures me, proving once again that he can read my mind, even without a magical bond. "And if you don't," he adds, slinging an arm around my shoulders, "you can always take over for me at the lumberyard."

"Ha ha," I reply, sending a sharp elbow into his ribs.

"Lighten up, princess." He tugs me closer, probably so I can't swing my arm enough to get in another jab. "You'll do fine."

"What, you're psychic now?"

"Didn't you know?" he asks seriously. "Must be an aftereffect of the bond."

I sigh. If only that were true. If only Daddy hadn't severed the bond fully and Quince still had some mer magic in his blood. If only.

I lean into his side, inhaling his scent of leather and mint toothpaste.

But I can't change the past. I just have to content myself with being with him here. Which isn't as rare as he seems to think. Ever since I returned to land, to high school, to Seaview, to *him* last week, Quince has been walking me to classes when he can and giving me rides to and from school on his charming death trap of a motorcycle. He's even stopped by a couple times to share milk and cookies when he gets home from his part-time job at the lumberyard. He's being a most devoted boyfriend—something I never would have guessed in the three years that he tortured and tormented me at every turn. Who knew he secretly loved me?

I'm a very lucky girl.

And the best part? He thinks he's a very lucky boy, too.

We've just made it into the hall that leads to my classroom and the boys' locker room when the rumble starts.

At first it's just the sound, a deep, low roar that sounds like the Earth itself is moaning. That startles most everyone in the hall and they stop, looking around, uncertain at this strange, unidentifiable sound.

Then we feel it. The ground beneath me starts to shake, kind of like when a wave comes in and pulls the sand from beneath your feet—except that I'm standing on linoleum tile, not a beach.

"What the hell?" Quince shouts above the roar and the shouts of panicked students.

The classroom door closest to us slams shut.

"I don't know," I reply, grabbing hold of his hand and squeezing. "It almost feels like . . . an earthquake."

The metal locker doors grind against their frames, and the fluorescent tubes above flicker with the movement.

This is crazy. Florida doesn't have earthquakes like this. Especially not *south* Florida. Hurricanes? Yes. Tornadoes? Occasionally. Swarms of killer sharks offshore? Unfortunately. But it doesn't have earthquakes, and certainly not ones this powerful. The entire school is shaking.

"Come on," Quince yells, pulling me toward the gym. "We need to get in a doorway."

We're not the only ones with that idea. Groups of terrified-looking students huddle under the beige metal frames of the four sets of double doors leading to the boys' gym. There's just enough room for us to squeeze into the last doorway.

I don't know how Quince knows what to do—I guess he's just that kind of can-do guy—or why a doorway is the best place to be, but I'm relieved. Land-based earthquakes are way beyond my realm of experience. I've been in a few underwater quakes. They're not at all the same. Mostly it's a lot of noise and heavier-than-usual current flow. If the epicenter is close, sometimes the ground vibrates a little. Our belongings might get swirled around, but our buildings don't shake. Nothing like this.

None of our settlements are built on fault lines, so we don't have to worry about what would happen if the epicenter were directly beneath Thalassinia.

They might be feeling the effects of this quake, though. The kingdom isn't that far offshore. If the school is shaking around me, who knows how far out the tremors are radiating? I should send a messenger gull when I get home, just to check in.

"Maybe it's a bomb," a terrified freshman next to me whimpers.

"Or a terrorist," her friend says, gasping. "It could be an attack."

"It's not an attack," I say, trying to calm them down without rolling my eyes at the melodrama.

Quince leans around me and gives them a reassuring smile. "It's just an earthquake. It'll be over in a——"

Before he finishes, the roar quiets and the ground stills.

The hall goes eerily quiet, everyone frozen in an aftershock of confusion. Even the lights above have stopped flickering. I'll bet Seaview High has never been this silent during school hours ever. Then, after half a second, the hallway explodes in noise and chatter as still-freaked students hurry on to their classrooms.

Quince says, "That was——"

"——weird," I finish.

Quince and I stand there, hand in hand, for several long moments, like we're waiting for something. For the other shoe to drop, maybe. The fire alarm or a tsunami or just another quake. It doesn't seem like this sort of thing could just . . . be over.

After a couple minutes, it seems obvious that it was a one-time thing.

The PA system squeals to life, blasting from the speakers in the hall ceiling. "All students, please proceed to your seventh-period classrooms immediately. Seventh-period teachers, please print out your attendance sheet and send it to the front office when all students have been accounted for." There's a squeal—they really should have Ferret, the news team sound guy, check out the mic—and short pause, followed by "Teachers with an open seventh period, report to the principal's office for further instruction. That is all."

"You okay?" Quince asks, his voice sounding a little odd.

"Yeah," I reply, reluctantly letting go of his hand. "We'd better go."

"I'll meet you right here after seventh." He presses a quick kiss to my lips before turning and heading into the gym.

I hurry to my study hall classroom two doors down, wondering if everyone is feeling as unsettled as I am.

The administration spends the first half of the period continually reassuring the students that everything is fine, that Seaview is fine, and that classes should continue as usual. Which is difficult, considering the semiconstant interrupts by the blaring PA system. When Brody shows up in the doorway twenty minutes before the final bell, I've only managed to read one (really short) paragraph of *A Separate Peace*.

"Hey, Coach Parsnicky," Brody says to my study hall supervisor. "I need to steal Lily away."

Parsnicky, coach of the freshman girls' basketball team, shrugs and waves vaguely at me and then at the door. He doesn't even look up from his playbook long enough to see the yellow pass in Brody's hand.

"News team?" I ask, slipping a heavily doodled sheet of notebook paper into the book to mark my spot and then shoving the book into my backpack. I like the book well enough, but I'm relieved I don't have to try to reread another word right now.

Brody nods, giving me that charming smile that used to make my heart flutter and my legs buckle. Now I just smile back. It's funny how much things can change in a matter of days.

"Principal Brown wants us to do a special report about earthquake safety for Monday announcements," Brody says as we step into the hall. "Everything's great, don't panic, obey all traffic laws."

"Basically everything they've been broadcasting for the last half hour," I reply. School security propaganda.

"Pretty much."

In my time as the news team cameraperson, we've done almost fifty special reports. Most of them are fluff pieces about school dances and sports stars. A very few are what Brody calls Seaviewgates, uncovering things like unfair grading scandals and faculty criminal records. (Madame Elliott was subsequently cleared of all charges, by the way.) And the rest of our reports are school-sanctioned announcements that the administration thinks will actually stop locker vandalism—aka spray paint—and parking lot rage.

They have virtually no effect whatsoever.

I don't mind the fluff pieces—I'm just the eye behind the camera anyway—but I'd love it if we could do some actually useful segments. Interviewing marine biologists about ocean warming. Or maybe an exposé about illegal offshore dumping, which happens more often than the general population knows. Or even some tips about water conservation. Something that might mean something to the world.

When we reach the studio, Ferret and our CGI specialist, Amy, are already prepping the equipment.

"I've got our cameraman," Brody announces.

"Camera*woman*," I correct, slinging my backpack onto the floor from the door and crossing to the video camera. It's pointed at the green screen, where Amy can add whatever background the newscast needs.

"What's the plan?" I ask as I remove the dust-deflecting cover from the camera and power it up.

"Just give me a minute to tweak Principal Brown's script," Brody says, dropping into the chair behind the computer and opening the file. "We don't have much time to pull this together. Lily, can you set up the teleprompter?"

We all dig into our duties, and as I set up the teleprompter for Brody, I think about how lame this safety speech will be, even after Brody fixes it. We should really be reporting on the causes and effects of the quake. Why waste the students' time when we could, you know, *educate* them instead?

"Brody," I say, turning away from the teleprompter, "I have an idea."

"What's that, Lil?" he asks, not looking up from the screen.

"What if we trimmed Principal Brown's safety speech," I

suggest, "and add on an expert interview?"

Brody actually looks up at me. "Who do you have in mind?"

"I don't know," I admit. "Maybe one of the science teachers? Maybe—"

"Miss Molina." Brody jumps to his feet. "She teaches earth science."

"And she's the Environmental Club faculty sponsor," I add.

"Perfect," we say at the same time. Two weeks ago I would have taken that as some kind of cosmic sign. Today I just think we're on the same page for once.

"Amy, pull up the interview backdrop." He heads for the door. "I'll go get Miss Molina. Have everything ready when we get back. This is going to be a bell chaser."

Yeah, we're going to cut it close on time.

He disappears into the hall and the rest of us scramble to get everything into place. By the time he returns with Miss Molina in tow, we're ready to go.

"Hi, Miss Molina," I say, waving from behind the camera as Brody gets her situated for the interview.

"Hello, Lily," she replies with a smile.

I was in her class freshman year. She inspired me to sign up for the Environmental Club, but once I joined the news team and became swim-team manager, I didn't have time. Considering the reason for my choices—spending time with Brody—I kind of regret not sticking with the Environmental Club.

"Okay," Brody says, adjusting his body mic. "Ready."

Ferret does the countdown, I start recording, and the segment begins. There's no time for clever angles and splicing cuts, so I just leave the camera on a wide view and let it roll. I listen eagerly as Brody asks a few mundane questions about the sources of earthquakes and why scientists can't predict them.

I don't usually interrupt his interviews because he's pretty intense about the process, but I can't help asking, "What about the effects offshore?"

"What do you mean?" Miss Molina asks, turning to face me.

I glance at Brody, expecting a dirty look for stealing the focus, but he looks intrigued.

"Um, I mean," I stammer, "if we felt the quake so strongly on land, then surely it was felt in the ocean, too."

"Most likely," Miss Molina answers.

"Then what kind of effects will it have on ocean geology and sea life?" I feel a little self-conscious, especially since I already know the answers. The students of Seaview probably don't, though. And maybe they should. "Do earthquakes cause the same kind of destruction underwater as they do on land?"

"Not usually," she responds, speaking directly to the camera. "The vibrations, which cause so much damage up here, are absorbed by the water."

"How interesting," Brody says, wresting the interview

back into his control while sticking to the new direction. "Tell us more about underwater quakes."

I smile behind the camera, content to watch Brody go after the topic with his usual determination. For the next ten minutes, he quizzes Miss Molina about earthquakes and plate tectonics and undersea land shifts with the agility of a seasoned reporter. I throw in a couple more questions, when the interview slacks, but for the most part Brody is masterful.

With only a few minutes before the bell, he calls the shoot a wrap. I hand him the video disk, and he heads to the editing station with Ferret to pull together the final cut. I shut down the camera and start to strike the teleprompter.

"Can I have a moment, Lily?" Miss Molina asks.

Her serious tone makes me a little nervous, but I say, "Sure."

I carefully coil the cable that connects the teleprompter to the computer.

"I was very impressed with your knowledge of underwater geology," she says. "You plan on going to college?"

"I do," I answer. "*If* I get in. My grades aren't great and I still have to take the SATs."

She reaches into her purse and pulls out a green paper. "Do you know what school you'd like to attend?"

"Whichever one will take me," I say. Slacker mer princesses can't be choosy.

"You should think about Seaview Community," she says,

handing me the paper. "Their admission requirements are not as stringent as at the four-year colleges, but their classes and professors are first-rate. I'm actually a graduate of the marine biology program."

"Really?"

"Don't tell anyone earth science is only my second love." She nods at the paper. "They offer a summer internship program for incoming first years. Unpaid," she explains, "but terrific experience."

I skim over the paper. According to the bullet points, students accepted into the program are set up with internships at the aquarium, the zoo, or a local scientific firm. That's a huge opportunity for anyone who wants to go into marine biology. Which I just might. I need a career now, and that one seems like a perfect fit. The program has a special concentration in marine ecology and conservation. That would give me a chance to help Thalassinia, even if I'm not the queen.

The paper also says that students must demonstrate sufficient interest and aptitude for the field, as well as having both practical and educational experience.

Well, that takes me out of the running.

"I don't think I have enough experience," I insist. "I've only had one year of biology, and I haven't been in Environmental Club since freshman year."

"That's more than most of their applicants will have," she argues. "I can guarantee you a good chance at acceptance into the program and a tuition scholarship."

"How?"

"Because I can see you have a passion for the field," she says. Leaning back, she smiles. "And I have brunch with the program director every Sunday."

"That's—" I shake my head. "Wow."

"If you're seriously interested," she says, "I could set up an interview for you."

"That would be awesome, Miss Molina."

"How about next Saturday?" she suggests. "Denise is free in the mornings, and you could swing by her office on campus."

I do a quick mental calendar check. "Next Saturday would be perfect."

"Great," she says. "I'll set it up. Meanwhile, you go online and research the school and the program."

"Absolutely!"

I shake my head in awe as Miss Molina walks away. Talk about a perfect situation. Me studying marine ecology. Working to protect the oceans from up here on land. I shove the paper into my backpack, promising myself I'll go online tonight and check out the program's website.

The school bell rings, sending me scurrying to clean up. I finish with the teleprompter and then help Ferret put away the sound gear. We're just locking the sound cabinet door when Brody finishes his edit.

"Done!" he announces as he clicks the send button,

shooting the digital video to Principal Brown's email account for approval so it can run during homeroom Monday morning.

We give one another a round of high fives and then grab up our bags. I flung mine farther than the rest, so I'm the last one left in the classroom.

"I figured you'd be in here," a deep voice says.

Quince! I turn and find him leaning in the doorway, arms crossed over his chest and an amused smile on his face.

He lifts his brows. "I thought we were meeting outside the gym."

Damselfish.

He's teasing, but I still feel bad. I completely blanked.

"Sorry," I say, hurrying over and slipping my arms around his waist. "I lost track of time. Miss Molina was telling me about the marine biology program at Seaview Community."

"Oh, yeah?"

"She's going to set up a meeting for me with the head of the program. She thinks I have a good chance of getting in and getting an internship and a scholarship."

"That's great." He slips a hand beneath my backpack strap, pulls it off my arm, and slings it onto his shoulder as we leave the classroom.

I hope I haven't made him late for work.

Quince and I fall into a comfortable silence as we walk to his motorcycle and then on the ride to our street. All in all, it's pretty handy having a next-door boyfriend. Especially when he has transportation.

He pulls into the shared driveway between Aunt Rachel's house—my house, too, I guess—and his, purring his bike to a stop.

I climb off and remove my pink helmet.

"How late are you working?" I ask.

His arm darts out and around my waist, tugging me closer. "Until eight."

I make a little pouty face, but I'm not trying to guilt him or anything. I don't begrudge his job at the lumberyard. Not only does it help out with his mom's expenses, it also helps out with those strong muscles that are holding me against his side right now.

"You'll stop by after?"

He raises up and presses his lips against mine. "Absolutely."

I'm tempted to sink in to him and collect on the promise of more kisses, but I don't want to make him later than he already is. He missed a bunch of work the last few weeks because of the time we had to spend in Thalassinia to get our separation. He and his mom can't afford the lost pay for being late.

You might think I'd regret choosing to sever the magical bond that formed between us when Quince gave me my first kiss, four weeks ago. At the time, though, it was the only choice I could make. I wasn't sure of my feelings, I didn't trust them, and I wasn't about to ask him to make a lifetime commitment on a hunch. He would have been tied forever to me and Thalassinia, forced into whichever body form I was in for the rest of his life. That's a lot to ask for a land-loving guy with a struggling single mom who relies on his help and his paycheck.

And now that I'm sure of my feelings . . . well, I guess I'm still glad about the separation. If we'd stayed bonded, I'd probably be in Thalassinia right now, performing some kind of boring princess duty or tedious ceremony or critical judgment. Part of me belongs on land. An even bigger part of me belongs with Quince. The rest of me is terrified of the kind of responsibility that comes with becoming crown princess or—worse—queen. Yep, I'm happy with my choice.

"Go then," I say, giving him another quick kiss. When he starts to wrap his other arm around me, I twist out of his grasp. "Later."

He breaks into a grin. "See if Aunt Rachel will make those key lime bars again."

"Is food all you think about?" I tease, shoving against his shoulder.

"No," he replies, all serious. "Sometimes I think about football."

He twists the throttle and is backing down the driveway before I can smack him again.

"Careful or I'll request the prune pistachio balls!"

Not one of Aunt Rachel's greatest cookie experiments.

He laughs, that deep, unrestrained laugh that makes me shiver all over. As he roars off down the street, I watch until he turns the corner and disappears from sight. Oh, sigh.

When Aunt Rachel gets home from the pottery studio at seven, I have all the ingredients for key lime bars spread out on the counter. I am in no way prepared to actually attempt this recipe by myself. Electronics are my friend, but cooking is not. The one time I tried to use the oven without supervision I nearly burned off my eyebrows. Lesson learned.

I've also finished my homework (except for trig, which I'm saving to do with Quince), so I quickly clear my books and notebooks into my backpack. Prithi meows in annoyance as I step away from the table, taking my toes out of licking range. Since the day I arrived, she hasn't been able to resist licking or nibbling or rubbing against me at every opportunity. I wonder if mergirls are irresistible to all cats, or just to Prithi.

"What's for dessert tonight?" Aunt Rachel asks as she drops a paper shopping bag and her always overflowing tote bag—filled with magazines, art supply catalogs, shawls, aluminum water bottles, and who knows what else—on the bench by the kitchen door.

She amazes me. Even after long hours at the studio, she still has a smile on her face and a bounce in her step. She is a woman of both boundless energy and unending generosity. Sometimes I step back and think about our situation, and I wonder how she managed to handle taking in a brand-new teenage niece without breaking stride for a second.

I guess it's a testament to her take-things-as-they-come attitude. I don't think I'll ever deal with change as well as she does. Especially not on an empty stomach.

Even from halfway across the room, I can smell the take-out. My belly grumbles at the thought of food, but I tell it to wait.

Aunt Rachel inspects the array of ingredients on the counter. Smiling, she picks up a bright green lime. "Key lime bars again?"

I nod with a grin. "By special request."

I invited Quince to start stopping by after work because hours of hauling and lifting and cutting and loading always leave him famished. His mom works at night, so she leaves a reheatable dinner in the fridge. Now when he gets home, he grabs the container from his fridge and then comes over to eat dinner and cookies. Aunt Rachel and I have always made treats—well, she makes treats and I assist. It's not much trouble to make plenty to share.

We always make extra treats for him to take home to his mom. Quince is practically family, so she is, too. Besides, Aunt Rachel is always very generous with her kitchen.

"Let's get them in the oven." She takes one of the pair of matching homemade aprons, a pale water blue covered with a rainbow of sea life—she let me pick the fabric, obviously—and quickly knots the neck and waist ties into bows. She hands the other apron to me. "Once they're baking, we can eat dinner. Italian takeout."

Mmm.

Fifteen minutes of sifting, mixing, crumbling, and spreading later—with Prithi circling my feet the entire time—the bars are in the oven and Aunt Rachel and I are settled in at the kitchen table with plates full of ravioli and breadsticks. Bread, by the way, is one of my favorite land foods. We can't exactly bake up a loaf in the ocean. Lots of water. No fire. No bread. And on the scale of breads, Italian breadsticks—all soft and warm and drowning in garlic and butter—are at the very top.

I'm just sighing into my third one when Aunt Rachel asks, "Anything interesting happen at school today?"

She forks a bite of mushroom ravioli into her mouth.

I swallow my bite of breadstick. "You mean besides the earthquake?"

"Heavens." Aunt Rachel practically chokes. "The studio was so busy tonight I'd forgotten. Is the school all right?"

"Everything's fine," I reply. I push a chunk of breadstick around in the sauce. "News team had to make a special announcement for Monday's homeroom broadcast."

"It's so strange," Aunt Rachel says. "They were interviewing a seismologist on the radio, and he said the apparent epicenter is not near any known fault line."

"Did they say where?" I ask. Not that I'll know anything. Despite a full year of earth science with Miss Molina, I'm still pretty clueless when it comes to land-based geology.

"Yes." Aunt Rachel swirls ravioli through her sauce. "About forty miles off the coast. Just west of Bimini."

"What?" I choke.

"Bimini," she repeats. "It's the westernmost island of the Bahamas."

"I know what Bimini is," I explain. "It's in the eastern part of my kingdom."

"Really?" Aunt Rachel takes a sip of her iced tea. "Are earthquakes common in Thalassinia?"

"No," I reply, confused. "Not really."

Most of the underwater quakes in the region hit farther south, around the Dominican Republic and Puerto Rico. Tremors in Thalassinia are more like the once-every-few-centuries kind of thing. The last one recorded by our people was about two hundred years ago.

And even then, the quakes aren't strong enough to be felt on the mainland.

"Do you need to send a messenger gull to the palace?" she asks. "To make sure everyone's all right?"

"Yeah, maybe." I shake my head. "We're not anywhere near a fault line, so I don't see how the epicenter could be so close."

Abandoning my ravioli, I head to the window above the sink and slide it open. I make a gull sound into the night, knowing that no ordinary gull would ever respond to my sad excuse for a call. Moments later, a big gray-and-white seagull flies into the kitchen and lands on the counter.

I pull open the junk drawer and grab the pad of kelpaper I keep there just in case. As I scribble a quick note, just asking Daddy if everything is okay and whether he knows anything about the quake, the gull notices the dinner on the table.

"Oh, no, you don't," Aunt Rachel warns, waving her fork at the hungry bird.

I snip a piece of twine and tie the note to the gull's leg before he gets himself forked for going after our dinner. "Take this to King Whelk of Thalassinia, please."

The gull gives one last longing look to the table full of food before flying back into the night. Daddy will have my note within the hour, and hopefully I'll have an answer shortly after that.

I sit down and resume chewing my ravioli in silence, thinking about all the consequences that *might* have swept our way on land as a result of this huge earthquake. Tsunamis. Mud slides. Whole stretches of the south Florida coast sucked into the sea.

Thankfully, none of this happened.

If huddling in a doorway with Quince and filming a special news report were the worst of the damages, then it was hardly a blip on the disaster scale. Plus I found out about the internship.

"You know Miss Molina?" I ask.

"Wasn't she your earth science teacher?"

"Yep," I say, pushing away my empty plate and grabbing

for a fourth breadstick. "After we finished the special report, she told me about an internship program at Seaview Community. She thinks I might be able to get in."

"That's wonderful, Lily," she says, patting my hand. "What kind of internship?"

I give her a quick rundown of what I know—which isn't much, I guess, but I'll know more after I study the website and then meet with the director next Saturday. "I might be able to get a scholarship, too," I add. "Which would be nice, since my grades are garbage and my SAT scores aren't going to be much better."

"You're working on that," Aunt Rachel says. "Between your test-prep classes and your extra study hours with Shannen, I'm sure you'll do far better than you expect."

I hope so.

After I decided to come back to Seaview, to pursue a life on land, I met with the school counselor for the first time. She pulled up my records, read through my grades, and then gave me a very concerned look. With a GPA in the barely 2.0 range, she'd explained, I would have to do extremely well on the SATs or ACT to get into college.

Tests are not my best stroke. I'm far better in the water than I'll ever be in front of a book. But if I want to be anything more than a janitor at the aquarium, then I need college. My life on land needs to be at least as meaningful as my life as queen would have been. I don't think I'd make a great leader, but I do think I could make a decent marine biologist. I know the oceans better than any human, and I am personally invested in protecting and preserving them. If I can make the waters better and safer for my merkin, then my life on land will have served a valuable purpose. What more could a soon-to-be-former princess want?

A sharp knock on the kitchen door washes away my thoughts. I jump up, thrilled. Quince!

Prithi chases after me, batting at my bare feet.

It's not until I'm pulling the door open that I wonder why Quince is knocking when he usually just walks right in. The huge smile on my face disappears as soon as I see who's standing on the other side.

2

"**W**hat are you doing here?" I demand.

"Nice to see you too, Lily," Dosinia says. "Miss me?"

Not hardly.

First of all, I left Thalassinia only a few days ago. I haven't had time to miss anyone.

Second of all, my bratty baby cousin hates me and is generally horrid whenever we're in the same place at the same time. Even if I'd been gone a decade, I couldn't miss her. That would imply I actually like being with her. Very much not the case.

"Why are you here, Doe?" I repeat, not bothering to hide the irritation in my voice.

It's not a complete and utter shock to find a merperson on land. They don't show up at *my* door, though, because of my royal status. They don't want to impose. But many merfolk visit the mainland occasionally—some frequently. Doe is not among them. Even if she didn't despise me, she usually wouldn't step out of the sea to save her best friend. She has a serious hate on for humans and avoids them like last week's red tide. Which makes the fact that she's standing on Aunt Rachel's back porch more than a little suspect.

"I thought for sure Uncle Whelk would send a note," she singsongs with fake sincerity. Pulling a square of pink kelpaper from her cleavage, she says, "Ooopsy. Guess I intercepted the messenger gull."

Pink kelpaper means it's a private message and the gull should deliver it only to the intended recipient—me. Leave it to Doe to get it anyway.

Jaw clenched, I snatch the note from her sparkly fingertips.

"Daddy will be pissed when he finds out you did that," I say, angry but secretly pleased to know she'll be getting into trouble for this stunt.

"Not any more than usual," she replies casually.

Prithi, apparently thrilled to realize I am not the only fishlike girl in the world, darts between my legs and begins rubbing her head against Doe's ankle. Doe glares at the cat and then rolls her eyes, as if deciding the creature is beneath her concern.

Like I said, Doe's not exactly a fan of land dwellers. Guess cats make the list, too.

Ah-hem. A discreet cough from behind me in the kitchen

reminds me that Doe and I are not the only ones present.

"Lily," Aunt Rachel says, "won't you introduce me to your friend?"

I almost blurt, "She is *not* my friend." But that's not fair. Aunt Rachel's never met Doe. In fact, she's never met any merfolk besides me and Daddy. Well, at least not knowingly. When merpeople are in terraped—human—form, the only thing that distinguishes them as children of the sea is the mer mark on the back of the neck. And even that can look like an ordinary tattoo if you don't know what you're looking for.

Anyway, a decade and a half of royal training sends me into social autopilot. I turn and smile.

"Aunt Rachel, this is my cousin Dosinia." Jaw clenched, I meet Doe's scornful glare head on. "Doe, this is my mom's sister, Rachel."

For an instant, an emotion flickers in her eyes. If I were looking at anyone but Doe, I'd say it was sympathy, compassion. But it *is* Doe, so it was probably just a speck of dust.

I sense Aunt Rachel moving up next to me. "We were just finishing dinner," she says to Doe, "but I'm sure we can find you something. I think I have a frozen pizza hidden away for just such an occasion. And there are a few breadsticks left from our takeout."

My breadsticks, I want to shout.

Not that Doe seems interested. The look that passes over her face as she takes in the remains of our dinner on the kitchen table is pure revulsion. I'll admit it took me a while to get used to human food. For my first few months on land, I survived on mediocre sushi and fresh produce. It was at least a year before I had the courage to try pasta. Now I love it.

Still, even though I understand that look, I'm defensive of human food. I am, after all, half human.

"It's good," I insist. "Don't knock it until you've tried it."

She gives me a confused scowl that says, What the heck are you talking about? Then, with a shake of her head, she says, "I'm not hungry."

As if that were the end of a very deep conversation, we all fall silent. An awkward tension fills the air. I don't think any of us knows quite what to say.

I'm wondering what Doe is doing here.

Maybe Doe is wondering the same thing.

Aunt Rachel probably just doesn't know how to react to finding another mer teen in her kitchen.

In the end, Doe breaks the silence.

"I've been exiled," she blurts.

"What?" I demand, my jaw slacking open. Of all the possible reasons for Doe's appearance on my doorstep, an exile would not have even made my list. "Why?"

Exile is the most extreme punishment in the mer world. The offender is banned from the sea, forced to live on land for the duration of the sentence. In other kingdoms it may be more common, but Daddy does not use that power lightly. In fact, I can remember only one exile in my lifetime: a merman who lost his mate, went mad, and tried to attack the palace by luring a group of great whites past our defenses. In his time in exile, he fell in love with a human and chose to stay on land to be with her.

I can hardly see Doe's exile ending like that.

"What did you do?" I ask.

She shrugs and nods at the note.

With a roll of my eyes, I carefully unfold the kelpaper crushed in my fist.

FROM THE DESK OF
KING WHELK OF THALASSINIA

Dearest Lily,

Your cousin has finally taken her hatred of humans too far. She must learn to move beyond her prejudice. To that end, I have sent her to you, exiling her and revoking her mer powers until such time as we decide she is ready to return. I am sorry to put such a burden on you, but I am sure you are up to the task. I would not have taken such drastic measures were the situation not desperate.

Yours,

Daddy

Exiled without her powers? She must have really crossed a line this time. Doe's spent most of her life breaking whatever rules she can get away with—and if it made my life miserable in the process, then bonus—and suffering the pretty mild consequences.

Quince thinks she's jealous of me and my soon-to-be-former title, but I think she's just a toadfish.

Still, until now her punishments have been more like cleaning out the palace kitchens or taking the algae-eating snails for a swim so they can empty their tanks. An exile is extraordinary. She must have done something truly horrible.

"What did you do?" I repeat.

Again, she shrugs. "Are you going to make me stand out here all night, or what?"

I give her a scowl that says I just might.

But Aunt Rachel doesn't know her like I do and steps around me to say, "Of course not, dear. Please. Come in."

Aunt Rachel throws me a glance that suggests she's not too pleased with my manners. She doesn't see the gloating look on Doe's face as she sweeps into the room.

"Doe . . . ," I warn.

She ignores me. Turning to Aunt Rachel, she hands her another piece of kelpaper. "Uncle Whelk sent a note for you, too."

Aunt Rachel gives her a questioning look before unfolding the paper and reading Daddy's scribbled note. When she looks up, her eyes are bright like she might be on the verge of tears. "Of course," she says, stepping forward and pulling a reluctant Doe into a warm hug. "Of course you will stay here while you're on land. There's a guest bed in my sewing room, and it's yours as long as you need it."

Whatever Daddy wrote must have struck just the right chord with Aunt Rachel.

"What did the note say?" I ask her. "Why has Doe been exiled?"

She gives me a sad look and shakes her head. "He didn't say." Then, turning back to Doe, she says, "I'll go get your room ready."

Before I can blink, I'm left alone in the kitchen with Doe, with Prithi purring dutifully at *her* feet—the furry little traitor—and less than no clue about what's going on.

Aunt Rachel's voice drifts back from the stairs, "Take the key lime bars out of the oven when the timer goes off." Her voice grows fainter as she reaches the second floor. "Don't forget to use the pot holders."

"I only did that once," I mutter. Burn blisters on both palms were more than enough to teach me that lesson.

"So this is where you live?" Doe asks with a sneer, sweeping her piercing blue gaze over Aunt Rachel's kitchen. "Kind of a drift downstream from the royal palace."

Her evaluation makes me look at the kitchen with fresh eyes. Like when I first walked through that door three years ago.

Aunt Rachel had met me at the beach, where Daddy tearfully passed me off to Mom's sister. He stayed completely kingly about the whole thing, though, dismissing the tears as a bit of seaweed in his eye. Aunt Rachel had driven me home in her beat-up station wagon—my first time in a car—and let me into the house through the kitchen side door. The look on her face had been one of nervous expectation. She'd been worried about what I would think of her home, like I might not think it was good enough after living in the Thalassinian royal palace for so long. She shouldn't have worried. I took one look at the sunny yellow cabinets, sky blue wallpaper, and rustic metal hardware, everything worn but homey, and fell completely in love.

Everything about this house is brightness and warmth and love, just like Aunt Rachel. So the idea of someone looking disparagingly—that means belittling; I've been studying my SAT vocabulary—at the kitchen is beyond insulting. Especially if that person is Doe.

Squaring my shoulders, I step up to Doe until we're practically nose to nose. She's in my world now, and I'm immune to her fake charm.

"Listen up," I snap, so she knows I'm serious. "I don't know what you did to get sent here, and honestly I don't care." Okay, I do, but I'm not about to tell her that. "But know this: You can be your usually hideous self with me all you want, but while you are a guest in Aunt Rachel's home, you will treat her with respect. You got me?"

In typical Doe fashion, she just meets my angry glare head-on, unblinking. Unfazed. Unaffected.

"Because if you do anything to insult, disrespect, or otherwise bother her in any way"—I lean even closer—"then Daddy's exile will be the least of your worries."

Doe doesn't flinch.

As we hold our staredown, a blaring buzzer fills the kitchen.

"That'll be your key lime bars, then?" she asks with a cool smirk.

"Aaargh!"

Spinning away from her, I punch the timer and jerk open the oven door.

"Don't forget the pot holders."

Ignore her, I tell myself as I snatch the pot holders from their hooks above the stove. She's insignificant, like tiny little sea lice. I can't let her get to me. Especially if she's going to be here awhile.

Son of a swordfish, that would be awful. Doe is bad enough in small doses, let alone for an extended period of time. I'm not sure I would survive that.

I've just set the baking dish full of key-lime-bar goodness on the stovetop when the kitchen door swings open.

"Why, is that key lime I sm—"

Quince breaks off in the middle of his teasing question when he spots Doe standing in Aunt Rachel's kitchen. I adore seeing that look of utter shock on his face when *I* put it there. Not when it's Doe's doing.

"Dosinia?" he asks, sounding as confused as I am.

She drops her jaded, disenchanted facade and flings herself at him, shouting, "Quincy!"

It is only the questioning look he throws me over her shoulder that stops me from grabbing the still burning-hot dish of key lime bars and flinging them at her obnoxious back.

That, and the fact that I would be beyond disappointed if the bars were ruined before we got to eat even one.

"What are you doing here?" he asks, pulling her arms from around his neck so he can look her in the eye. "I thought you hated land."

"Not land," I say, circling around her to slip my arm proprietarily around Quince's waist. "Humans."

I smirk at her dark scowl.

Then, turning a shining smile on Quince, she says, "I've been exiled." She flicks a taunting look at me before returning her attention to my boy. "I'll be around a lot for a while."

Doe in residence is not what I need right now. As if the SATs and interviews and new boyfriends and graduations and a million other things weren't enough, Daddy had to throw my squid-brained baby cousin into the mix.

Just great.

"You don't know what she's like, Shannen," I complain. "Really, you don't."

Prithi, annoyed by the agitated movement of my feet, meows an echoing complaint. She spent the entire night crying outside Doe's door. I'm pretty sure she's only returned her attentions to me because Doe still isn't out of bed. I'm the only mergirl available.

"I can imagine," Shannen says, checking over my SAT sample test. "Lily, you spelled your name wrong."

"I'm distracted." I take the paper back from her and erase all those bubbled-in circles before filling in a fresh set. "You should have seen the way she flung herself at Quince. Like he was her long-lost best friend, when she barely knows him and I know for a fact that she hates all humans." Throwing Shannen an apologetic glance, I say, "Sorry."

Shannen waves me off, never one to dwell on an insult. "Maybe she's jealous," she suggests, echoing Quince's own interpretation of Doe's behavior.

Why does everyone think this? They don't know her as well as I do.

Shannen asks, "How long has it been since she had a boyfriend?"

"A boyfriend?" I echo. "Doe?" Never, maybe. Doe is more the love 'em, leave 'em, don't-bubble-message-me-I'll-bubble-message-you type. "I don't think she's ever gone out with the same boy more than a couple of times."

Shannen quickly scans my revised test, marking up more than half the answers with her red pen. "Then she's probably jealous of your relationship."

Snorting in disbelief, I try to imagine a world in which Doe is jealous of me. Nope. Doesn't exist. Although my relationship with Quince is completely enviable. Other than that, my life is pretty much murky. A big part of my future depends on a miraculously decent SAT score.

"Lily," Shannen groans. This is going to be bad. "The square root of 121 is not 121."

My head drops to the table. "I'm hopeless," I mumble against the painted white surface of the kitchen table. "I'm never going to get into college."

Even with the insider connection to Seaview Community, I still have to get a better-than-pathetic score on the SATs. I have to prove myself capable of academic success or something equally ridiculous. If only I could explain that school hadn't seemed that important for the last three years because I was going to return to Thalassinia to be crown princess after graduation. Now that I was staying, I would totally focus more on my class work.

But thankfully since the human world is still unaware that the mer world exists, I can't exactly provide full disclosure. Sometimes I think my life would be much easier if I didn't have to keep that part of myself a secret. It's a nice brief fantasy, but then reality returns and I remember why that's impossible.

Prithi laps at my toe, as if telling me she's perfectly content for me to stay right here forever. At least until Doe wakes up.

"You're not hopeless." Shannen grabs a fistful of my frizzy blond hair and tugs me upright. "You're just behind the curve a bit. Especially in math. Your writing and critical reading scores are much better."

"That's because we speak English in Thalassinia." At least I'm not from one of the Spanish, Danish, or Japanese-speaking kingdoms. I'd be toast. "If there was a whole test in marine biology, I'd ace it for sure."

"Don't worry," Shannen says, her voice full of a determination that might be the only thing between me and a life of fast-food jobs. "We'll get you in shape before the real deal in two weeks."

"Two weeks?" I squeak. My head falls back to the table.

"You just have to focus," Shan explains. "Tune out other distractions."

Easier said than done.

Until I decided to give up my crown and live on land indefinitely, college had been the furthest thing from my thoughts. I'd stick it out through graduation, just long enough to make Brody fall in love with me and go with me to Thalassinia when high school was over, so I could take up my duties as crown princess. That had been the extent of my future planning.

Now, there's Social Security numbers and paperwork and a five-year plan and more things than I can possibly keep in mind at once. And that's just the future stuff. There's also the new boyfriend, my eighteenth-birthday ball, and the renunciation.

If I want to help my kingdom from above, through human

channels, then I need to succeed. I need to do well on the SATs and get on the college track, or I'll wind up watching my marine biologist plans float away.

Still, I'm not giving up. I'm a Thalassinian princess, and we're made of strong stuff. If I need to focus and remove myself from distractions, I can do that.

"How do you sleep on that contraption they call a bed?"

My short-lived optimism vanishes as Doe—aka Very Big Distraction—walks into the kitchen.

Abandoning my apparently less-tasty feet, Prithi pounces at Doe's hot pink toes. Doe ignores her.

I glare at Doe. "You'll get used to it."

It had taken me several weeks to adjust to sleeping on a flat surface rather than the curved shell-shaped beds we use in Thalassinia. But now I adore all my fluffy hibiscus bedding and being able to curl up on my side with the covers pulled tight around me. It's like being stuffed in a cozy clamshell.

"I won't be here long enough to get used to anything," she retorts.

She's still being vague about the details of her exile, avoiding any and all questions about what she did to get sent here.

"And just how long *will* you be here?" I ask, watching nervously as Doe surveys the room.

Her gaze lands on Shannen. Ignoring my question, she asks, "Does this one live here, too?"

I feel my land temper burning my cheeks. If we were

in Thalassinia, the water would calm me until I was only mildly annoyed. But since we're on land, I'm instantly on the verge of furious at her snide question about Shannen. No one disparages my best human friend.

"This *one*," I growl, "is Shannen. A very good friend. She's helping me study because that's the kind of thing friends do." Under my breath, I add, "Not that you would understand anything about friendship."

"Nice to meet you," Shannen says, offering Doe her hand.

Doe, of course, stares blankly at the hand before rolling her eyes and stalking into the room. Prithi is fast on her heels. "Where can a mergirl find a glass of kelpberry juice in this place?"

Typical Doe. Walking in like she owns the world, treating everyone like sludge, and expecting them to cheerfully serve her. Well, if she thinks she can pull off that attitude on land, then she's in for a very harsh lesson. One I'm not going to teach her. She can sink or swim on her own in this world—I'm not going to be her guiding current. I've got my own life to get in order.

Ignoring Doe—and Shannen's questioning look—I hunker over my study guide and reread the directions for the math section for the fifteenth time. (Note: They still don't make sense.)

I'm trying to interpret the meaning of the obscure instructions when Aunt Rachel sweeps into the room.

"Good morning, girls," she says, her long, flowing skirt

fluttering behind her. "Hard at work already?"

"Yes, Ms. Hale," Shannen replies.

Aunt Rachel's stopped asking Shannen to call her by her first name. She's practically family—especially now that she knows my big, fin-shaped secret—but she can't seem to shake a lifetime of respect-your-elders training.

"Good morning, Dosinia," Aunt Rachel says, setting her newspaper on the table and heading for the coffeemaker. "Did you sleep well?"

Doe snorts.

The fine hairs on the back of my neck, just above my mer mark, stand up. I force myself to take a deep breath and release some of my fury on an exhale. It's a technique I learned from Quince, and I'm going to need it if Doe is here for more than a day or two.

Especially if she keeps insulting my nearest and dearest.

With my jaw clenched, I snarl, "You didn't even give it a ch—"

"Would you like some juice, dear?" Aunt Rachel asks before I can scold—er, explain to Doe about her inappropriate behavior. "There's a pitcher in the fridge and glasses in that cupboard."

Doe's gaze follows the wave of Aunt Rachel's arm to the refrigerator and then stops. "The *fridge*?"

"Don't you have refrigerators in Thalassinia?" Aunt Rachel asks, sounding truly intrigued. Then she laughs at herself. "No, I don't suppose you would need them."

"On land we need to keep things cold," I explain before Doe can spit out the biting comment that's already sneering across her lips. "So they don't spoil."

To save us all from some sort of incident, I shove back from the table and stomp to the cabinet. In Doe's defense, this world is completely foreign to her. Not that ignorance excuses her rudeness.

"This is a glass," I explain, holding one up for her to see. We have glasses in Thalassinia—which is why Doe rolls her eyes at me—but they're not for juice. Since everything back home is surrounded by liquid, juice wouldn't stay in a glass for long. We have bottles for things like kelpberry and sand strawberry juice. I jab the glass into her hand and then pull open the fridge. With the pitcher of orange juice in hand, I pour a generous amount into her glass. "It's orange juice."

"The juice of an orange?" she asks, sounding confused.

It's not that we never have oranges in Thalassinia—we do a lot of trading with land-based merchants and have a pretty astounding variety of land-grown produce. Especially at the palace. But we only ever eat oranges in segments. No one ever thought of juicing them.

"Yes," I answer sharply. "Orange juice."

All of us watch expectantly, or maybe fearfully, as Doe cautiously takes her first sip of orange juice. It's a small sip, barely enough to give her a real taste, but enough for her to decide what she thinks about it.

It's like we're all holding our breath, waiting for her

reaction. I'm not sure why Aunt Rachel and Shannen are so expectant, but I'm bracing myself for a Doe-style explosion. A tirade, maybe, and orange juice flying across the room.

Never one to live up to expectation, Doe betrays no emotion. Just shrugs and takes another sip.

I'm not sure whether to smile or scowl.

"If everything is all right here," Aunt Rachel says, pouring her coffee into a car mug and tucking her newspaper under her arm, "I'll be off. I have an early class at the studio."

"Fine," Doe says with a sunny smile. Totally fake.

Prithi meows contentedly as she circles Doe's ankles.

"Yeah, I need to go, too," Shan says. "Promised Mom I'd help her clean out the garage today."

She shudders as she gathers up her things.

I give her a pleading *do-you-have-to?!?* look.

"Keep working through the sample test," she says, pushing the book toward me. "I'll call later to check on your progress."

Moments later, Doe and I are alone in the kitchen, with only Prithi's pleased purring interrupting the tense silence. In a completely negligent manner, Doe holds her glass over the sink, twists her wrist, and lets the juice pour out. The look on her face dares me to say a word.

Oh, I've got more than one.

My anger needs to wait, though. First, I need to find out why she's here.

"Dosinia," I say, trying to sound stern while keeping the rising anger out of my voice, "why exactly did you get exiled?"

She shrugs as she sets the glass on the counter. "I have no idea. I certainly didn't do anything *wrong*."

"Nothing wrong?" Wrong, in this case, I suppose, being up to Doe's own interpretation. No one gets exiled for doing nothing wrong. "Daddy wouldn't exile someone for no reason. Especially not a merperson of royal descent and especially not with revoked powers."

Revoking a merperson's powers is even more serious than exile. That means Doe can't breathe underwater, can't transfigure, and can't control the temperature of liquids. She can't use any of the personal magical powers that make us mer. She's still a merperson and subject to the rules and magic of our people, but as far as anyone can tell, she's completely human.

That must bug the carp out of her.

Fine. If she won't tell me why, then she can at least tell me how long.

"So you're exiled—for no reason whatsoever," I say, with a heavy dose of sarcasm. "And without your powers. How long will we be stuck with you?"

She shrugs again. "Uncle Whelk didn't say."

My teeth grind slowly together. "Then what *did* he say?"

Pulling back a chair at the table—the chair that neither

45

Aunt Rachel nor Shannen had been using, as if she might get human cooties from them—she seats herself directly across from me. "He said you have to teach me to fit in here, in Seaview."

Is that all? Well, if Daddy had to give me a task, at least this is an easy one. Fitting in has never been a problem for Doe. Although she can be—and usually is—a total sea witch, she's not a social leper or anything. She's beautiful, and boys fall over their fins to please her. In Thalassinia she's pretty popular. Shouldn't be too tough to translate that into Seaview terms.

The biggest difference will be the clothes. She didn't bring anything with her, so at the moment she's wearing the tank top she swam here in and finkini shorts made from hot pink and purple scales. Daddy must have left her just enough magic to maintain her modesty. Some of my clothes might fit her, but her curves are definitely, um, curvier than mine.

I'm not exactly eager to share with her, but I can make do for a few days.

"Don't like my outfit?" she asks with a sneer when she notices me evaluating her attire. "You used to dress just like this. Then again, you used to be a mer princess."

I ignore her jab. "Your clothes aren't exactly land appropriate."

"Here." She tugs a small pouch from her deep cleavage

and drops it on the table. "Uncle Whelk sent this to cover my expenses."

I tug open the drawstring pouch to find an eyeful of pearls. Beautiful white, cream, pink, and even a few rare black pearls, all in perfect condition. These will fetch a significant amount.

They will cover a lot of expenses.

"How long do you expect to be here, Doe?" I ask. The money we'll get for selling the pearls would pay all of our household expenses for a month. "When do you get to go home?"

Her gaze drops to the table, and she absently rubs at the scratch I made in the paint the first time I tried to make frozen pizza. Some of her attitude ebbs, and I see, for the first time, that she's just as uncertain about this situation as I am.

Sometimes she makes it too easy to forget she's just a sixteen-year-old kid.

"I don't know," she admits. "Uncle Whelk said I needed to stay here until I learned to appreciate humans."

Great. For Doe that could mean never. Not that I completely blame her, of course, given her history, but it's a semi-impossible task.

"Did he say how to determine if you've succeeded?"

"He said you would make the call." She looks up, her blue eyes glowing with unshed tears. "You decide when I've learned my lesson."

"Well, that's easy," I say, jumping up, uncomfortable with her sudden display of emotion. "You stay here a few days, hang with my friends, act like you don't want to kill them all with a death ray from your eyes, and we'll be good to go."

Even before I'm finished, she's shaking her head slowly.

"He also said to tell you," she whispers, "to consider this your final duty as princess of Thalassinia."

Duty.

With that one word I drop back into my chair. It's the one word that can completely sink me. I've been raised my whole life to appreciate the responsibility of my position, to understand that duty comes before almost everything. And even though Daddy encouraged me to follow my heart—which means giving up my place in the succession—that sense of duty is not so easy to dismiss. And if Daddy is calling on my sense of duty to deal with Doe, then that means I have to see it through to a legitimately successful conclusion.

It also means that whatever she did to get exiled is really, really bad.

"Oh, Doe," I say sadly, shaking my head. "What did you do?"

I don't expect an answer, and she doesn't give one. But I know there's no way I can give her an easy pass. I have a feeling there's more at stake here than just my inconvenience.

Settling in on Doe's toes, Prithi lets out a sad wail.

My feelings exactly. Well, if Daddy thinks it will serve Thalassinia to help Doe get over her human hate, then that's what I need to do. Because responsibility is difficult to ignore, and until my eighteenth birthday I am royally bound to fulfill my duty. Whether I like it or not.

"Let's get you dressed," I say, pushing to my feet. "We're going shopping."

3

onday morning, Aunt Rachel drives me and Dosinia
to school. Quince gave me a kiss when I told him I
wouldn't be riding with him on his motorcycle and promised me another one when I meet him at my locker. That
will have to sustain me.

While I've become a fan of his motorcycle—kind of—
sometimes I wish one of us had a car. His mom needs
her clunker for work, just like Aunt Rachel needs her
station wagon. On days when the Seaview weather verges
on hurricane-force winds or torrential tropical downpour,
a vehicle with a roof would be a definite advantage. Not to
mention the fact that we could be on our way to school
together right now, with Doe safely in the backseat—or
maybe the trunk—rather than him roaring off on Princess
alone and me stuck listening to Doe whimper the whole ride.

Until I get a job or Quince starts working full-time, it's

motorcycles and borrowed rides for me.

"It's fine," I explain to Doe for the twentieth time since Aunt Rachel turned the ignition and put the station wagon in gear. "Just think of it as a wakemaker on wheels."

The wide-eyed, nostrils-flared look Doe shoots at me indicates she is not thrilled with the analogy. I'm surprised her death grip on the back of my seat hasn't punctured the worn upholstery. I'm even more surprised that Doe is allowing this break in her I'm-too-cool-for-everything facade.

She must really be freaked out. For a girl who can swim at a rate of almost fifty knots, you'd think a quick cruise through a residential area would be no big deal. I will admit that Aunt Rachel drives like she's commanding a high-powered race car instead of a rattletrap station wagon, but I've gotten used to it. Mostly I just close my eyes.

By the time we pull into a visitor parking spot near the Seaview High front entrance, Doe's practically a statue. I climb out onto the sidewalk, my backpack slung over my shoulder, and grab the handle on the back door. She doesn't move when I swing it open.

"You can get out now," I explain, hiding the fact that I consider her terror a little entertaining. "We're here."

The look of grateful relief on her face washes away my joy. It's the same look I see on my best friend Peri's face after a near-encounter with a jellyfish. Definitely no laughing matter.

I've never seen Doe look so vulnerable.

"Grab your bag and come on," I say, uncomfortable with these soft feelings for my squid-brained cousin. "Aunt Rachel's going to get you registered."

Dosinia climbs out of the wagon on shaky legs, her new briefcase clutched in her fist. Yes, a briefcase. I couldn't believe it either—I mean, how *un*cool can you be—but she said she couldn't stand the feel of the straps from backpacks and messenger bags. I tried to explain Seaview social law to her, but she didn't care. Typical.

Everything else about her is trendy perfect. A flowy-yet-curve-hugging purple tunic, black leggings, and knee-high black leather boots. Her stylishly straight caramel blond hair, makeup that would make a Hollywood stylist proud, a big (fake) diamond-encrusted starfish hovering just above her cleavage. She's on land one weekend, and she has more style than I've developed in three years.

Sea witch.

"You girls wait out here," Aunt Rachel says as we reach the front office. "I'll get things taken care of in a jiffy."

As we sit, waiting, on a vinyl-covered bench in the front hall, I evaluate my own lack of style. A brown ruffle-tiered skirt that falls just below my knees. A lime green tank top with little gold bits sparkling around the neckline. Gold ballet flats that Doe practically forced me to buy. ("You might as well get something out of this deal," she said. Then, with a judgmental once-over, "And you can definitely use the help.")

Today's selection is not horrible as far as outfits go. It's when you get to my head that things go awry. Frizzy blond hair I can never hope to control and face devoid of all makeup save lip gloss, because attempts at anything more result in pure disaster.

How is it that my human-hating cousin manages to pull off the movie-star look and I still look like I'm fresh off the boat? For three years I've blamed it on some mystical human-girl knowledge that no mergirl could ever hope to obtain. Now I have to admit that it's just me. I'm style challenged.

"So this school thing lasts, what?" Doe asks. "A couple hours?"

I try not to laugh myself right off the bench. "Look, I know you're used to the relaxed schedule of the royal tutors, but this is a whole different thing."

I give her a quick rundown of how school works on the mainland—seven hours of classes, homework after hours, sports and other extracurriculars. If I know Doe, she'll jump up and be out the door before I can say, "Truancy is a punishable crime." Doe thinks responsibility is a four-letter word.

But she just slouches—fashionably—against the wall, crosses one leg over the other, and starts humming the Thalassinian national anthem. "No big," she says. "I've been on an advanced study track for the past year."

She can't be serious. When I still lived at home we had lessons together with the royal tutor. Being two years apart, we were never studying the same thing, but she always seemed beyond bored and wholly uninterested in academic learning. I wasn't much better, I know, but Doe doing advanced studies? That's ridiculous.

"What do you mean, an advanced—"

"Morning, Lil." Brody emerges from the front office, looking like his carefree, charming self. "How are you?"

Forcing the Doe-induced scowl off my face, I smile. "I'm great."

"Did you get the email about the news team meeting after school?" he asks. "It's time to start planning our graduation coverage."

I forget all about Doe and her advanced study track. News team calls.

"Not yet. When did it go out?" I ask, shaking my head.

It took me a while, but I've finally got the hang of using the computer. We don't have much—okay, anything—in the way of electronic technology in Thalassinia. Water and electricity don't exactly mix.

But I'm mostly computer literate.

"Just now." He jerks his thumb toward the office. "I was showing Principal Brown how to see the final earthquake safety video and managed to sneak a peek at email."

"I'll ask for a computer-lab pass in homeroom so I can check."

"Don't bother," he says with a charming grin. "We're

meeting in the studio after school. That's all the email said."

"What's an email?" Doe asks.

Next to me, Doe looks Brody up and down before focusing her attention on his golden brown eyes. Oh. No.

All of a sudden, life drops into slow motion. I see Brody's attention slowly shift around me to Dosinia's—fashionably—slouching form. Doe bats her heavily mascaraed eyes at him, each bat taking three full seconds, I swear. Her glossy pink lips purse out into an extra pout.

On my other side, an even more charming smile spreads across Brody's lips.

Warning, Lily Sanderson. Danger approaching.

Brody steps around my knees to stand in front of Doe, on the pretext of making a polite introduction. I feel like I'm watching a school of tuna swim into a gang of great whites, but I can't look away from the inevitable feeding frenzy. Not when there's nothing I can do to stop the catastrophe. I feel completely helpless.

"Hello there," Brody says, the words drawn out in my slo-mo world. "I'm Brody."

Even though Doe hasn't moved an inch, there's something about the tilt of her eyebrows, the pull of her mouth, that tells me she is quite interested in the specimen of boy standing before her. Whether they're human or not, she's boy crazy on an incomprehensible scale.

Doe has never been afraid to go after what interests her.

55

And she usually gets it.

When she sits up, holds out her elegant hand, and says, "I'm Dosinia," my world finally bursts back into normal speed.

"She's my cousin," I explain, jumping up to stand between them. Desperately clutching for the cover story we've agreed upon, before she slips up and reveals our fishy secret, I say, "She's here as an exchange student. From the Bahamas. Just swam in this weekend. I mean flew, of course. *Flew* in. We picked her up at the airport."

Brody accidentally found out I was a mermaid once before. I had to mindwash him, and although I think it worked perfectly, it gave me a roaring migraine. I'd rather not have to do that again anytime soon.

Oblivious to my panicked babbling, Brody leans to his left so he can see around me and makes the kind of eyes at her I've only ever seen him give his ex-girlfriend. When she wasn't quite as ex as she is now.

No, no, no, no, no. This is bad. Brody's a girl hound and Doe's boy crazy. Bad, bad, *bad* combination. Especially when I glance back over my shoulder and see her flash him a seductive smile.

I have to do whatever I can to keep these two apart. Besides the fact that Doe hates humans—cute boys included—and that Brody's mind has been washed—by yours truly—to make him *forget* mermaids really exist, the idea of my baby cousin and my ex-crush hooking up is just . . . *wrong*. In every possible way.

Desperate to derail this collision, I start to suggest, "Why don't we—"

"All set," Aunt Rachel announces, pushing out of the front office, thankfully saving me from whatever lameness I was going to invent. "No problem with your, um . . ." She casts a wary glance at Brody. ". . . records."

Meaning that the records Daddy's royal scribe forged to give Doe a land-based background and an academic history have passed administration muster. We did the same thing when I first came here.

"Here is your class schedule." Aunt Rachel hands Doe a computer printout. "You have economics first."

Before the terrified thought can even form in my head, Brody says, "Me too! Let me walk you."

He grabs Doe's briefcase off the floor and does that chivalrous-guy thing where he holds out one arm toward the hallway, indicating that she should precede him in the direction they're going. Brody's being chivalrous. Doe's being . . . Doe. This can't end well.

"This is bad," I mutter as they disappear down the hall. "This is really bad."

"She'll be fine," Aunt Rachel says, laying a reassuring hand on my shoulder.

"I hope so." But my I'm not holding my breath. "Because

a messy situation between Doe and Brody could make last week's earthquake look like a slight drizzle on the scale of trouble storms."

Just call her Hurricane Doe. Category Five.

I guess that makes me the emergency response. Any trouble Doe causes is ultimately my responsibility, my final duty as princess of Thalassinia. I'll be the one on the floor with a sponge and a bucket.

By lunchtime I'm a nervous wreck. Doe and I have not had a single class together—which isn't surprising, since she's enrolled as a sophomore—but besides knowing that she and Brody both had econ this morning, I found out they also have the same homeroom and fourth-period typing class. All that unsupervised time together, who knows what might have happened.

Maybe I'm overreacting. Maybe Brody just walked her to class and they haven't spoken since. Maybe flying fish will hop up on land and start salsa dancing. Still, it doesn't hurt to be cautious.

Straining to see over the sea of bodies in the lunch line, I hunt for the blond and brown-haired pair in the cafeteria. But there are so many heads in my way, I can't even get a good view on tiptoe.

"What are you looking for?" Quince asks.

I growl in frustration.

"Dosinia," I mutter. "I think she has her eyes set on Brody."

"Well, that's not great," Shannen quips.

How observant. "Duh."

I try to jump, hoping to propel myself above the crowd while not spilling my trayful of lunch. My box of milk ends up on the floor.

Quince, who's brought his lunch as usual and is only keeping us company in line, bends down and retrieves my half pint. "Why are you so worried?"

I throw him a you've-got-to-be-kidding look. But when he doesn't shake his head and say, "Omigosh, you're right," I lean close and whisper, "Think about what happened with us."

His lips spread into a very-pleased-with-himself smile. "Nothing wrong with that."

"Now imagine that happening between Doe and Brody."

He shrugs. "Still not seeing the problem," he says. "Your cousin is nice enough, and Benson's not completely void of redeeming characteristics."

"Bennett," I snap. "And that's not what you said two weeks ago."

"Two weeks ago I was trying to keep your eyes off him, princess."

"Well, you were right before." I try another jump and land on Quince's foot. "He's a shallow, self-absorbed jellyfish."

"I'm confused," Quince says. "Are you looking out for Brody? Or for Dosinia?"

"Both of them," I half shout. Why is he being so dense about this? He knows all the possible complications that might ensue if anything happens between them. "The two of them hooking up is bad news no matter which way you look at it."

Shannen nods in girlfriend solidarity and says, "Prime-time trouble."

With a shrug, Quince strains up to see over the ocean of students around him. With a few inches on me, he easily scans the room.

"They're at a table together," he says, coming back down to my level. "Want me to go out there and join them?"

"Uh-huh." I nod my head vigorously. As he heads off into the crowd, I shout after him, "And save us seats."

As Shannen makes it to the cashier, she says, "I know you don't like your cousin, but is she really that bad?"

"You have no idea."

"Would she really kiss Brody?" she asks as she hands over her money.

"I hope not, but with Doe it's impossible to say." I move my tray forward when Shan picks hers up. "I mean, she hates hum—" I jerk back, realizing what I was about to say in a room full of humans. "Well, you know. So that's a point in the favor of sanity."

"But . . . ?" Shannen prods when I've collected my change and my tray.

"But," I say, leading the way between the lunch tables toward Quince's dark blond head, "Doe is boy crazy and unpredictable. And she's always been a little reckless. Consequences don't mean much to her."

"A very bad combination."

"Oh, yeah." We reach the table and I slide onto the seat next to Quince. Across from Doe and Brody, who are sitting way too close together for my nerves. "Hi! How's your first day going?" I ask, maybe too brightly.

"Fine," she replies, not sparing me a glance.

Brody, however, does. "Doe's been telling me some great stories," he says with a big, teasing smile.

"I'll bet she has," I answer with a growl.

Doe flashes her who-me-I'm-innocent eyes at me. As always, there's hint of mischief in them.

Quince places his warm, reassuring hand on my knee. Silently saying, Don't freak out. Too late for that. I reach down and lace my fingers through his, squeezing out my frustration on his hand.

"Doe says you're an amazing swimmer, Lil," Brody says, leaning forward. "How come you never tried out for the girls' team?"

I squeeze Quince harder. I can't exactly tell Brody it's because I'm only a good swimmer in my mer form. The tail fin is a big boost in the underwater-speed department. With legs, I swim about as well as a rock.

"It's the competition," Shannen says, coming to my rescue. "It stresses her out and she practically drowns."

Doe snorts.

Quince laughs.

I squeeze until I think Quince might lose all blood flow to his fingers.

"Yeah," I say, going along with the explanation, since it's just about as believable as anything else I could come up with. "I don't do well under pressure. I faint. I have to settle for being swim team manager."

"Besides," Doe says, finally chiming in on the conversation, "Lily only swims in the ocean. She's allergic to chlorine."

I force a laugh. Throwing her a dark look, I say, "That too."

She's cutting it a little too close to the truth.

Mermaids aren't just allergic to chlorine. It's toxic to us. If you want to call human susceptibility to arsenic an allergy, then yeah, I guess I'm allergic. A quick dip in a public pool wouldn't kill me, but it would make me really sick. If I tried to stick it out for an entire swim practice, though . . . well, let's just say that I wouldn't have to worry about my SAT prep anymore.

Quince, apparently realizing he's in danger of losing his fingers—which would make working on his motorcycle really hard—reaches over with his other hand and pulls off my death grip. But instead of withdrawing completely, he sandwiches my hand between both of his.

"I'll bet Lily has some great stories about Doe, too," Quince says. "Don't you, princess?"

For half a second I'm confused. Every single Doe story I have is an underwater one. He knows I can't dish that dirt.

"*Don't you*, princess?" he repeats.

He looks me in the eye and winks and I finally get his meaning. After growing up together, I know plenty of things Doe probably wouldn't want me to share. I don't have to actually *tell* the stories, just hint at them enough so Doe knows I won't be bullied by her. She's not the only one who can tell embarrassing tales.

And I know the perfect tale to not tell.

I bolt up straighter.

"I do." I throw her a warning look. "I have a whole *treasure* chest of stories."

Her eyes flash. I know she knows exactly what I'm talking about: the time our cousins Kitt and Nevis made a fake treasure map and she spent two days scouring the Thalassinian garbage fields for a buried chest of rare pink diamonds. She was only about eight, but she is still mortified by her gullibility.

As if conceding that if we're going to play hardball, I might not win, but I won't go down without a fight, she gives me a slight nod.

Score one for Lily.

The table falls into a vaguely tense silence. I think we all realize that lunch is almost over and we've barely touched our food. I take this moment of silence to see what Doe has on her tray. She (wisely) passed on the meat du jour, a grayish hamburger with wilted lettuce, instead opting for strawberry Jell-O, vanilla pudding, and a banana. All foods similar to ones we have in Thalassinia.

I think part of her human education needs to be about trying new foods. Sushi may top my list of all-time favorites, but I've developed a taste for corn dogs, tater tots, and apple pie. And you haven't lived until you've tried tiramisu.

Maybe educating Doe in human ways won't be all that bad.

After all, it *is* my duty. And if I get to consume some of my favorite foods in the process, then all the better. Tomorrow I'll have to get some extras on my plate to make her try. I'm pretty sure it's taco day.

"Gotta run," Brody says, pushing to his feet and picking up his tray. "We're doing oral reports in history today and I need to review my notes." He nods down at Doe's picked-over tray. "Have you finished?"

She makes a kind of disgusted face and pushes her tray away.

"I'll take this up for you." Brody stacks their trays and winks at Doe. "See you later."

Her gaze doesn't leave him until he drops off the trays

and disappears out the cafeteria doors. Her interest in Brody is a little too interested for my peace of mind.

Before the human food lessons, I have to make one thing very clear. I will not let my final act as royal princess end in a bonding disaster that can only bring trouble to my kingdom.

As soon as Brody's out of sight, I say, "No."

Doe looks innocent. "No what?"

"No Brody," I explain. "Absolutely, unequivocally no."

She shrugs. "Whatever."

I'm not sure if it's an I-don't-really-care-about him-so-no-big-deal shrug, or an I-like-him-and-I-don't-really-care-what-you-think one. Or maybe it's a you're-not-the-boss-of-me shrug.

"Dosinia," I say, not willing to let this go, "this is serious. You can't mess around with Brody. I don't know if I told you, but he accidentally found out the truth about me a couple weeks ago."

"So?" she asks in a bored tone.

"So he didn't take it very well. He acted like a jerk and I had to—"

"Ancient history." She reaches down and grabs a lip gloss from her briefcase, swiping it perfectly across her lips without a mirror.

Grrr. I can envy her makeup skills later; right now I'm trying to make a point. "You can't mess with any *human*, Doe. The risk is too high. Think of what's best for the kingdom."

"Like you do?" she snarls, her voice full of venom. "When have you *ever* put Thalassinia first?"

My head jerks back at her verbal attack. "What do you mean?" I ask. "I take my responsibilities very seriously."

She snorts. "Right."

"Doe, I—" I'm not sure what to say. Mostly because her accusation hits home. Because these are doubts I already have, doubts I've been wrestling with ever since I made the decision to return to Seaview.

Am I abandoning my kingdom by staying on land, by staying with Quince? Am I letting my ancestors and my subjects down if I give up my title? Is it enough to try to protect them from above, rather than lead them from below?

I can't let these doubts consume me. I've made my choice, and Daddy supports me fully. There isn't another way to make things work that doesn't leave me miserable for life. Besides, I can help more on the environmental front from up here.

"The kingdom will find another heir." I shake my head, still trying to figure out where her attack came from. Whispering so no one around us can hear, I say, "Thalassinia will be better off without me."

Beneath the table, Quince pats my hand, reassuring me that he's here if I need him. Shannen would come to my aid, too, but this is a moment between me and Doe, between merfolk.

Unimpressed by my assurance, she stands up and says,

"I've got to find my art class."

My shoulders slump. Of course she has art. My luck is pretty stellar when it comes to things like this. Of all the classes I could share with my squid-brained cousin who hates me and thinks I'm betraying our kingdom, it would have to be my favorite class. It wouldn't be my life otherwise.

Shannen and I exchange a look. Mine, I'm sure, is defeated. Hers is apologetic. She knows how much I love art, so she knows I'm bummed. As Doe collects her briefcase and stands, Shannen jerks her head at my cousin.

I know.

I take a deep breath.

"Wait," I say with no enthusiasm.

Doe doesn't respond, but she doesn't walk away. I hear her booted foot tapping impatiently on the floor. When I don't say more, she finally demands, "What?"

Closing my eyes and taking a deep breath, I say, "We have art, too." When Shannen nudges me in the ribs, I add, "We'll walk with you."

Doe drops her briefcase on the table, as if to say, Fine. I'll wait.

"I'll see you in trig," I tell Quince, leaning down to press a quick kiss to his mouth.

He lays his hand, the one he nearly lost to my frustrated squeeze, reassuringly against my waist. He whispers, "Play nice."

I growl at him. Me? It's Doe we should be worried about.

She's the cutthroat one. I'm always nice.

Well, maybe not *always*. I reconsider. Thinking back to how I treated Quince before I learned he had feelings for me and before I figured out that I had feelings for him, too, I admit I'm *almost always* nice.

"Let's go," I say, snatching my tray off the table. "I don't want to be late. Again."

4

*B*y Thursday morning I'm so stressed out that I accidentally boil my orange juice, have to run back
upstairs and put on flip-flips that actually match, and realize
five minutes before leaving for school that I've completely
blanked on my American Government homework—which
is, of course, my first class, so I won't have homeroom time
to do the work sheet.

"Aaargh!" I slam my now-frozen juice on the counter. "I
can't take much more of this."

Aunt Rachel doesn't pretend to misunderstand my
meaning.

"I know it's difficult adjusting to a new member of the
household," she says calmly. Placatingly. "But it's just a matter of time."

I spin to face her. "I don't *have* time," I complain. "The
SATs are in a week, and I haven't been able to study at all.

Graduation is a month away. My grades are pitiful. If I don't do amazing on this test, then it's good-bye college, good-bye career, good-bye future."

Good-bye becoming a marine biologist and any hope of helping my kingdom from land. All my sacrifice will be a waste.

"You're overreacting."

"I'm not," I insist. "You know what the counselor said when I told him I'd decided to go to college. Well, after he finished laughing."

Aunt Rachel puts her newspaper aside. "I know, dear." She wraps a reassuring arm around my shoulders. "But I also know that putting all this pressure on yourself isn't going to help the matter."

I slump. Because she's right. Humans deal with stress poorly enough, but mermaids—a species with little stress in their natural habitat—don't process it well at all. Combine that with the added agitation of being out of the water for long periods of time and the fact that I'm sharing a bathroom with my drawer- and mirror-hogging baby cousin and, well, it's amazing I'm able to function at all.

"Everything will be fine," Aunt Rachel insists. "You'll do the best you can on the SATs, and who knows, you might do great. Besides, you have the interview with the director of the program at Seaview Community. You will be amazed by what a face-to-face meeting can accomplish."

My mood brightens, and I'm about to ask if she really

thinks so when she adds, "No matter what happens, we'll figure things out." Her voice drops to a more serious tone. "That's what life is. Facing challenge after challenge and figuring out a way to get through."

I take a deep breath. I know what her change of tone means.

Between us we've already faced a lot of challenges, like she's faced figuring out how to go on after losing a sister—my mom—and I've faced having to grow up without a mother. And then there was the challenge of finding myself magically bonded to a boy I thought I hated but who really turned out to be my perfect mermate. That one turned out rather well, by the way, so maybe not all challenges are all bad.

Right on cue and reading my mind as always, Quince swings open the kitchen door and walks in. "Morning, Aunt Rachel," he says, giving her a respectful nod. Then he turns to me. "Lily."

Yes, that particular challenge turned out pretty much perfect.

I launch myself at him. Arms around his neck, cheek against his shoulder. I'd probably be planting one on his lips if Aunt Rachel weren't standing right there. He slides his arms around my waist and rests his chin on my head. I send my worries downstream for a while, sinking into the comfort of his embrace.

"Good morning, Quince," Aunt Rachel replies. "Did you eat?"

I feel him shake his head. "Missed the alarm the first few times."

"I'll fix you some peanut-butter toast."

"I wouldn't put you out," he says, slipping into the southern-gentleman mode he seems to save for my relatives, "but my stomach would be most appreciative."

"I've missed you," I say, leaning back but not releasing him. "We've barely seen each other since Doe showed up."

I know he's feeling it, too. There's a hint of longing in his eyes, and somehow I know it's about me. Moments like this make me daydream, make me wonder whether there's a teeny-tiny filament of the bond still connecting us. I ignore this thought, which invariably leads to a vain hope that Quince can one day return to Thalassinia. That's something I can't think about right now.

He grins. "Let's change that this afternoon. I can take off from work and we could . . ."

He trails off when I give him a sad look.

"I can't," I explain. Why do the important things always seem to be in conflict? "I have an SAT prep class after school. It lasts until six."

Quince knows how much getting into college means to me, now that I'm going to be staying on land. He's been nothing but supportive of my desperate efforts to improve my chances at decent scores. But I also know he wishes we were spending more time together.

"How about this weekend?" he asks.

"I have that interview on Saturday morning." I release him so he can take the peanut-butter toast Aunt Rachel offers him. "After that I'm totally free."

He pulls out a chair at the kitchen table and takes a bite of toast, consuming almost half the triangle in one chomp. He nods while he finishes chewing. "Sounds good." Holding the rest of the triangle in front of his mouth, he says, "I thought we might take a ride down the coast," before the toast disappears into his mouth. "You've never seen the Keys, right?"

"Nope, never," I say.

I glance at Aunt Rachel for approval. She's usually pretty tolerant with me, letting me have my freedom and independence—one of the perks of having a hippie holdout for a guardian—but sometimes she puts her foot down. Like about last year's state swim meet.

Managers aren't invited to go unless the entire team qualifies. Since only Brody and one other swimmer from Seaview made the cut, my official presence was not required in Orlando. I wanted to go anyway, though, to support the team. And to spend quality time with Brody, of course.

Aunt Rachel had said absolutely, unequivocally, one thousand percent not on your life. She couldn't leave the studio for that long, and she wasn't about to let me go, unchaperoned, to another part of the state with no one officially looking out for me.

The fact that I'd have been practically alone with my crush probably didn't help my argument.

I'd been devastated, but in retrospect, I know she was right.

This trip is different. I think. It's not overnight and it's not Brody. Also, I'm older by a year and she adores Quince. She's been pretty vocal about how glad she is we're together. Hopefully this translates into trusting him enough to take me on a mini road trip.

When she nods, *whew*, I say, "Sounds like fun." I drop into the chair next to him at the table. "I miss riding on your motorcycle."

He gives me a surprised look—because I used to hate Princess, aka the beastly death trap on wheels. My first couple motorcycle-driving lessons didn't end real well, but being a passenger is way different. I love the feel of the wind in my face and my hair whipping behind me. It's like swimming in air.

Since getting a ride from Aunt Rachel that first day to get Doe registered, though, the toadfish cousin and I have been walking to school. No room for two passengers on Princess, and no way am I leaving Doe to her own devices. Who knows what kind of trouble she could find on her way to school.

"You can get over that," Doe declares as she walks into the kitchen, Prithi faithfully at her heels. "I've got a ride."

Quince waves at Doe, his mouth full of toast.

"What do you mean," I ask, "you've got a ride?"

Doe looks just as fashionable as she has all week in an

ankle-length skirt that changes from a deep purple at the bottom to almost white at the waist, a plain white tank top, and a big, silver multichain belt that hangs low over her abdomen. Even her briefcase doesn't distract from the fact that she is obviously a cool girl.

Three days on land and she's at the top of the social ladder.

How does she *do* that?

Plus she's managed perfect makeup, perfect silver manicure, and perfect, nonfrizzed hair. Life is so unfair.

"Brody's picking me up," she explains as she pours herself a glass of grape juice, which she's decided is a tolerable substitute for kelpberry juice. She turns to face me, glass in hand. "He didn't want me having to walk *all* the way to school again."

All the way? I snort. It's six blocks.

As much as I'd like to ride to school with Quince and not spend the extra fifteen minutes each way in dedicated one-on-one time with Doe, the idea of her and Brody alone in his car sends off warning bells.

"You can't ride with Brody," I say.

Doe downs her glass of juice before asking, "Why not?"

"Why not?" I echo. I'm starting to feel like a broken record about this. Does she really not get it? Or is she just trying to drive me insane? Both are viable options at this point. "Because he's a human. Because you're not. Because you're only going to be here a short time—"

75

"Because you still have feelings for him?"

I jerk back at Doe's accusation. "What? No," I answer after a heartbeat of shock. "Of course not."

I glance at Quince. I mean, he must know that I'm totally over Brody, right? Because I am. The only boy who gives me butterflyfish in the stomach anymore is Quince. I'm ruined for other boys. I know that's a cliché, but it's true.

He just kind of shrugs and rolls his eyes at Doe's suggestion, chomping the last bite of his toast. He has his mildly jealous moments, but I guess this isn't one of them. Brody isn't a threat anymore.

Doe sets her glass in the sink. "Then I don't see what the problem is."

"You don't?" I push to my feet. "It's just . . . well, you . . . and he—"

I look helplessly at Quince and Aunt Rachel, hoping that one of them will know how to get through to Doe. Quince shakes his head, and Aunt Rachel actually says, "I don't see the harm."

Am I the only sane person who sees this as a shipwreck in progress?

"Then it's settled," Doe says. A loud *honk, honk* blares from the direction of the driveway between our house and Quince's. "That'll be Brody. See you later."

She grabs her briefcase and heads out the kitchen door. Dazed, I follow her, leaning out the door to watch her climb into Brody's Camaro. He has his arm over the passenger seat, and when Doe sinks into the leather he tries to lean in for a kiss. Before I can shout "No!" she pulls back and laughingly pushes him to his side of the car.

Well, at least there's that. She's not entirely without sense.

I can't imagine what kind of disaster it would be if she let him kiss her and they wound up bonded. D-I-S-A-S-T-E-R. On a melting-polar-ice-caps scale.

"This isn't going to end well," I mutter as I turn back into the kitchen.

Quince is there, wrapping his big, strong arms around me.

"Things could be worse," he says.

"I don't see how."

"Well," he says, leaning back to give me a cocky grin, "I could make you *drive* Princess to school."

As much as I want to stay in a bad mood, I can't help but giggle. "Yeah," I concede. "That would definitely be worse. For everyone."

Quince winks. "Especially Princess."

"I'm off to the shower," Aunt Rachel announces. "You kids have a good day at school."

When the sound of her footsteps on the stairs fades away, Quince asks, "Is she gone?"

I peer over his shoulder, through the kitchen, and into the hall beyond. Before I'm done nodding, his lips are on mine. He gives me one of those long, soft, warm-all-over kisses that make me forget Dosinia and Brody and the SATs and anything that isn't just enjoying this moment.

Ah, yes, I mentally sigh. Everything will be fine.

Seven hours of school plus three hours of test prep equals complete brain fry. I'm pretty sure the goal of the SAT class is to teach me how to improve my score, but right now there are so many four-syllable words and mile-long equations floating around in my head that I can barely think straight, let alone actually make sense of test questions.

If I took the test right now, I'd probably score a negative number.

For once I'm thankful for the walk home. Except for my nightly saltwater baths—which I've needed more than ever since Doe arrived, go figure—this walk is the first quiet time I've had in weeks. It should feel good to be alone with my own thoughts for a while. But as the whirlpool of test prep seeps slowly out of my brain, other thoughts flow in. Like worrying about my interview on Saturday. And Doe's impossible interest in Brody. And the whole renouncing-my-title thing.

Maybe it's Doe's presence, or the knowledge that I'm carrying out my final royal duty, but for whatever reason, thinking about the renunciation is getting harder and harder. I've made my choice, and I know I can do a lot to protect Thalassinia here on land. It's still sad to think I won't be Princess Waterlily anymore. I suppose it's natural to have doubts about any major change. That doesn't mean I'm making the wrong choice. It just means it's a change.

Besides, I tried the alternative—giving up land and Quince and Aunt Rachel for a duty-filled life under the sea—and I couldn't stand it. I've made the only choice I can.

With each step on the faded concrete I try to pound all those troubling thoughts out of my head. I can't do anything about my worries right now. And dwelling on them will only lead to more stress and possibly an ulcer. Instead, I focus on the beautiful day around me, on the brightly colored flowers that line my street and the freedom of having time to myself. I focus on my breathing, thinking positive thoughts with every inhale.

Each lungful of fresh air feels like a crash of waves pounding the confusion out of my mind. The murk starts to settle and the waters clear. I look up at the sky, a perfect periwinkle blue—which makes me think of my best friend, Peri, and I wonder what she's doing right now, so far away. I'll see her again soon because her mom is making the gown for my birthday ball.

Between the ocean breeze and thoughts of Peri and forced positivity, I'm starting to feel revived. Refreshed, like the crisp calm after a storm.

The only thing that could improve the situation more would be a long soak in a key-lime-salty bath. The tub and I have a date later this evening.

When I finally get home, I feel like a brand-new Lily and

am looking forward to a post-school-and-test-prep snack. I think I've earned it. After bursting into the kitchen, I fling my backpack under the table and head to the fridge. There's a sticky note from Aunt Rachel on the door, reminding us that she has a late class today and won't be home until after eight. The good news is we're going to order pizza.

That will be a surprise for Doe.

She ignored me at lunch today and didn't speak to me in art. Her message was clear: I overreacted this morning about her and Brody. Maybe she's right. I should have more faith in her, I guess. She may be a boy-crazy toadfish, but she's not stupid and she's still a merperson of royal descent. Duty and responsibility have been drilled into her since guppyhood, too. Even if she usually chooses to ignore them. She's not going to accidentally reveal our secret or anything.

Grabbing a pair of cheese sticks from the fridge, I decide I need to apologize. If I'm going to teach her to not hate humans, I'm pretty sure she has to not hate *me* first.

String cheese is the perfect tension breaker and conversation starter—who doesn't love peeling the stick apart string by string?

And just in case that's not enough, I grab a pair of juice boxes.

Feeling optimistic, I bound up the stairs two at a time. When I get to Doe's door—the room that, until last Friday, was Aunt Rachel's sewing room—I kick gently at the base while pulling open one of the cheese-stick packages.

No answer.

Huh. I don't know where else she could be. I mean, it's not like she has extracurricular activities or an after-school job.

Besides, Prithi is staring intently at the crack under the door.

Doe must be in there.

"Doe?" I ask as I turn the handle.

Pushing the door open, my eyes scan the room for any sign of my cousin. As I look over the messy piles of clothes and the schoolwork strewn all over the floor and the unmade bed—Doe is clearly used to an extensive house-keeping staff—it takes me a few seconds to find her in the debris field.

Correction, to find *them*.

I get a view of way more Doe than I'd bargained for.

She and Brody are lying on her daybed, arms wrapped around each other, clothing still intact but bunched and disheveled to the point of revealing skin that's usually well and truly covered.

"Omigod!" I gasp.

I grab for the door handle, dropping the cheese and juice boxes in the process, and hastily pull the door shut, just as Prithi darts inside. That is something no girl should have to walk in on.

Heart pounding, I lean back against the closed door and

try to erase the mental image.

But no matter how hard I squeeze my eyes, it won't go away.

If only I could perform a mindwashing on myself.

I'm not sure how long it takes—two seconds? Twenty?—but all of a sudden it hits me. After blurring out the below-the-waist bit of the mental image, my focus shifts to their upper bodies. The part of the image at the top of her bed. Their heads.

My humiliation evaporates.

Fear and anger and utter panic flood my bloodstream as I whip around and throw open the door. It crashes against the wall and shakes the framed pictures of Mom's family.

"Dosinia Sanderson!" I shout.

She and Brody are now busy rearranging their mussed-up clothing, trying to act as if nothing at all was going on. As if I hadn't seen what I know I saw. Brody is on his feet, tugging his T-shirt back into place. Doe's pretty much put back together, skirt hem down where it belongs with no inappropriate skin showing, and is busy smoothing out her hair.

Too bad she can't do anything about her lips.

"What have you done?" I demand.

I can't tear my eyes away from her plumper-than-usual mouth.

Casually, as if she'd just accidentally spilled her grape juice on the kitchen floor, she swipes one finger beneath her bottom lip, clearing away any displaced lip gloss.

"What does it look like?" she replies with a smirk. "I'm making out with my boyfriend."

I don't know how I manage to stay standing. By all rights I should collapse into a heap on the floor, next to the piles of shoes and dirty clothes. I feel like I've been caught up in a powerful current that is dragging me . . . wherever it wants to go.

As it is, I have to brace my arms on the doorjamb to keep from pitching forward. Every awful thing I'd been afraid of happening just happened.

Doe kissed Brody.

And now they're bonded and Brody is turning mer.

D-I-S-A-S-T-E-R.

5

"Who's ready for pizza?" Aunt Rachel singsongs as she walks in the kitchen door. "I've got Lorenzo's on speed di—"

She freezes when she sees the three of us—me, Brody, and Dosinia—sitting around the kitchen table. I'm sure none of us looks terribly happy.

Brody, at least, has the grace to appear mortifyingly embarrassed. Good. He should feel like a froggin' clownfish after I found him making the moves on my baby cousin. And in my own house!

Not that I can be entirely furious with him. He doesn't have the slightest idea what he's gotten himself into—correction, what *Doe's* gotten him into. He's about to get the surprise of a lifetime, let me tell you.

Doe looks, as usual, unaffected. I might as well have only caught her sneaking an extra bowl of plumaria pudding before bed for all the guilt she's showing. She doesn't even seem to care what she's forced onto Brody, a boy she supposedly cares about.

I know she's only sixteen. I was sixteen once, and I remember what it felt like—the emotions and the desperation and the acting without caring about the potential consequences—but what she did . . . well, that makes every other teenage rebellion pale in comparison. She's not only screwing up her own life, she's screwing up Brody's, too.

And me? I can't see myself, but I've been clenching my jaw so hard for so long that my cheeks are getting cramps. My back is stick straight and my fingers are wrapped tightly around the seat beneath me—mostly to keep me from flying across the table and wringing Doe's unapologetic neck.

I just *knew* she was going to do something like this.

If we were underwater right now, I'm sure the sea would be boiling around me.

"Oh, dear." Aunt Rachel sighs, sinking into the empty seat at the table. "What happened?"

"We just—"

"Shut. Up," I snap at Doe. She has no right to speak at this point. She forfeited the right to defend herself when she *kissed a human!* Turning carefully and calmly—though probably more abrupt and furious—toward Aunt Rachel, I take a tight breath and say, "She. Kissed. Him."

Clearly, full sentences are not an option at this point.

Prithi meows at me from under the table, as if defending

her new favorite fish girl from my wrath. Turntail. She can go home with Doe if she loves her that much.

Aunt Rachel's gaze swings to Doe, who is pouting petulantly in her seat. "You didn't," she says sadly.

"I *caught* them." I turn my scowl on Doe.

Brody clears his throat. "Mrs. Sanderson, I—"

"It's Hale," I spit at him. He's magically bonded to a mergirl, and he doesn't even know her guardian's name. What was he thinking? Sure, the whole bond thing is not his fault, but he was an equal party in the kissing. He should know more about Doe than that she's hot. He just slid down another two notches in my estimation, and he didn't have too far to go before reaching the ocean floor. "Her name is Rachel Hale. *Ms.* Hale to you."

"Now, Lily," Aunt Rachel says, laying a hand on my forearm. "I know you're upset, but anger is not going to help the situation."

I flop back against my chair, jamming my arms across my chest. She's right, I know, but that doesn't mean I can magically send my anger away. That would take more bath salts than there are fish in the sea.

"What has the boy been told?" she asks me.

"Nothing," Doe says. "Lily hasn't let us—"

"I said, Shut. Up." I jump to my feet and start pacing. "For the love of Poseidon, you've done enough damage for one day."

"I know what we did was disrespectful," Brody says,

coming to Doe's aid. I begrudgingly give him points—one point—for that. "But it's not like we actually . . . you know."

"No," I say as I suck in a deep breath. "What you did was worse."

"You're being a little melodramatic, Lily," Aunt Rachel chides. "You know there is a solution to this problem."

I pace my way over to the kitchen sink, gazing out at the faded gray house across the driveway and wishing Quince didn't have to work so many late hours at the lumberyard. If he were here, then everything would be easier.

He and I went through this very thing just a few weeks ago—although, at the time, I'd thought it was Brody kissing me. I'd been in the throes of a three-year crush, so I shouldn't be held accountable for my actions. It was one big screwup from start to finish, but it worked out okay in the end. Quince is always far more levelheaded in crises—case in point, the earthquake. He'd know what to do, how to say it. Like a true princess. Prince. Whatever.

He isn't here, though. I'm on my own. I'll have to pull on my big-girl finkini and deal with the problem.

Putting it off will only make things worse.

Turning away from the sink, I lean back against the counter and face the table. Deep breath.

"There are a few things I need to explain to you, Brody," I say, hands gripping the edge of the counter behind me for support. "Are you ready for some earth-shattering news?"

Turning in his chair to face me, he looks confused.

This won't be easy. Until that kiss Quince and I shared a month ago, I'd never told a single human about my magical secret identity. Aunt Rachel already knew when I'd come to live with her three years ago, and everyone else . . . well, protecting my kingdom was far more important than sharing a juicy secret.

Now, once again, the revelation is unavoidable.

"First of all," I explain, clutching the counter tighter as if that will give me courage, "Doe and I are not exactly average human girls. We're"—I squeeze my eyes shut—"mermaids."

Silence washes through the room. I can't even hear anyone breathing. No movement, not even a meow from Prithi. Finally, when I can't stand it any longer, I force one eye open.

Brody hasn't moved. Even the expression on his face is still one of complete confusion. Clearly, he's in shock.

"Mermaids," I repeat. "We live in the ocean and can breathe wa—"

"I know." He shakes his head. "I mean, I know what mermaids are, but . . . I think I already knew that's what you are." After a quick glance from me to Doe and back again, he smiles. "Not about Doe, you know, but somehow I knew about you, Lily. I mean, I didn't know, but as soon as you said it, I felt like I already knew." He smiles wryly. "That doesn't make any sense."

Actually, it kind of does.

When the whole thing was going down with Quince a couple weeks ago, I decided to tell Shannen the truth. She is my best human friend, after all, and if I can trust anyone with my secret, it's her. Brody overheard the confession, and in that instant I realized I didn't want him to know. I didn't really love him.

So I performed a mindwashing to make him forget. It was my first—and, I hoped, my last—so maybe I didn't entirely erase his memory.

For a second I consider telling Brody about the mind-washing. No, maybe not. It's nothing bad, of course, but he might not be too happy about the fact that I'd messed with his memories. Who would be?

Not that it matters, because I'll just have to do it again as soon as he and Doe are separated. Nothing's changed in the last two weeks to make me trust him with the safety of my kingdom. Which brings me to part two of the revelation.

"The other thing," I say, bouncing nervously back against the counter, "is that a mermaid kiss isn't just a kiss."

"Oh for heaven's sake," Doe says, "stop swimming around the issue." She grabs Brody by the shoulder and makes him face her. "Our kiss ignited a magical bond, and now we're connected and you're turning into a merman. Are you cool with that?"

"Am I—?" Brody laughs. "What?"

"Doe!" I can't believe she just said that like that. No tact, no leading into the issue. Just *blam*, you're a merman. As my brain processes the last bit of her declaration, I jump forward. "Whoa! Brody is *not* turning into a merman."

"I'm not?" He sounds almost sad.

"I mean, you are," I amend. "Technically."

"Then what——"

"But we're not going to let it get that far," I say to Doe. "You're getting a separation just as soon as we can get you two to Thalassinia."

Doe's smile is positively evil. My skin prickles with a mixture of fear and anticipation. Slowly she turns in her chair, wraps a hand around her curtain of caramel blond hair, and pulls it out of the way. Prithi takes the opportunity to pounce into Doe's lap.

"I won't be going home anytime soon," she says, her voice laced with lava. "Remember?"

Her neck bared, I stare at the spot at the base where all merfolk are branded with the mark that makes them mer. But where Doe's two-part mer mark should be, only a hot pink kelpflower remains. The circle of waves around her mer mark is gone.

"Oh, honey," I gasp, losing my anger for a moment. "I-I'm sorry, I forgot."

That must have happened when Daddy revoked her powers. It's part of her punishment. The outer ring represents a merperson's aquarespire, our ability to live and breathe beneath the water.

I can't imagine losing that part of myself. Even though I've chosen to live on land, I still meet Peri off the Seaview pier a few times a week, and I still plan to visit Daddy at the palace every few weeks. I still feel the magical power of water in my nightly bath. I still get energized by the rain. I still *feel* mer in every way.

Being without that is unimaginable.

The line Doe crossed must have been really, really bad if Daddy felt the need to take the punishment this far.

Really bad.

"What does that mean?" Aunt Rachel asks. "Dosinia cannot enter the sea?"

I nod. "That's right."

"Oh, dear," Aunt Rachel says. "Are there any other options?"

The room falls silent for a heartbeat.

Before anyone else has a chance to think, Doe says, "I know." She lets her hair fall back into place. "*You* will have to take Brody to the palace."

"Me?" I stammer. "No, I can't. I have SAT prep and my interview and homework and college applications and, and, and—"

I look helplessly around the room, at three sets of eyes watching me expectantly. Okay, two expectantly, one gloating.

"Is there any other way?" Aunt Rachel asks.

"There must be," I insist.

I spend a few desperate moments racking my brain for any alternative. Maybe we could rent a submarine, or just a boat, and Daddy could swim up to the surface to perform the ritual. Or I could send a messenger gull to the palace and ask him to come to Seaview. That's when I know I'm defeated. I can't ask the king of Thalassinia to take a day out of his royal duties just because my schedule is kind of tight. Talk about unprincesslike behavior.

"There isn't," Doe says, her voice full of smug finality. "And you know it."

Slumping back against the counter, I know she's right. Doe can't return to Thalassinia until Daddy lifts her punishment, I can't ask Daddy to come here, and we need to get her and Brody separated as soon as possible. Definitely before next weekend's new moon. The last thing we need is the two of them feeling even more connected than they already do.

I mentally calculate my schedule for the next few days.

"It's too late to go tonight," I think out loud. Nightfall makes the ocean too dangerous to travel without an escort of palace guards. "If we leave right after school tomorrow, we might make it back here before midnight. Does that work for you, Brody?"

He shrugs. "I guess so." Then he laughs. "I'll miss a swim practice, but I can tell Coach I'll be doing an open-water swim."

"Brody . . ." I push away from the counter and approach him. "You know you can't tell anyone, right? No one can know our secret, or we all—you included—will be in serious danger."

"I know, Lil," he says, his tone uncharacteristically serious. His sober gaze flicks to Doe. "I wouldn't betray you guys like that."

"Good."

Surely he can keep a secret until tomorrow, until Daddy performs the separation and thorough mindwashing.

Maybe this D-I-S-A-S-T-E-R isn't as bad as I'd thought. Maybe it's just a Disaster. Or even a disaster. It can all be cleared up in one quick swim home.

I ignore the niggle of doubt that reminds me that that's what I thought *last* time. That quick trip home turned into a two-week, life-changing ordeal.

But that won't happen this time. Daddy has no reason to keep Doe and Brody bonded. Doe's not a royal princess who will lose her title if she's not bonded by eighteen. That's just me.

Soon this will be nothing but a bad memory.

"The change won't get too bad in one night," I explain. "If you start to feel dried out, drink a glass of salt water. And if it gets really bad, take a salt bath."

"Okay. . . ." Brody sounds like he's still in shock, and I can't blame him.

"Don't worry," I say, "it'll all be over before you know it."

He scowls, like he wants to argue with me. He doesn't get the chance.

The kitchen door swings open.

"Hey, I saw the light on—" Quince steps into the kitchen and, in a repeat of Aunt Rachel's earlier reaction, freezes on the spot. "What happened?"

"Hey, Fletcher," Brody says with a grin. "I'm turning into a merman. How cool is that?"

"Brody," I growl.

"Oh, sorry," he says. "Did he not already know?"

"He did," I say through clenched teeth, "but—"

"Then it's no big deal."

"Lily?" Quince sounds a little nervous. Or jealous.

"Don't look at me," I say, pointing at Doe. "I've learned my Brody lesson."

"Dosinia," he says, sounding like a disappointed father.

Doe rolls her eyes.

Just wait until *my* father hears what happened.

"I don't know about you kids," Aunt Rachel says, "but I'm famished. Who wants pizza?"

Everyone but Doe does. I'm so angry about her stunt, I forget about her human education. She can starve for all I care.

While we're waiting for Lorenzo's to deliver, I fix Brody a glass of salt water and focus all my energy on thinking positive thoughts about the quick trip to Thalassinia. I don't have time for things to go awry like last time. I really don't.

* * *

"Why do you think she did it?" Quince asks.

I look at him, barely making out his features in the waning moonlight. Two feet is too far away, so I scoot across the worn planks of his front porch until our shoulders touch.

"I have no idea," I finally say. "Who knows why she does anything? She's a toadfish who doesn't care about consequences."

A strong arm wraps around my shoulder and tugs me closer against his side. "I'm sure she has her reasons."

I sigh. "That's what I'm worried about." Losing your parents at a young age must lead to all sorts of behavioral issues. Her parents died in an awful fishing-boat accident when she was nine, and she's been a bit of a rebel ever since. Doe always does whatever she wants to do, for reasons that make sense only to her. Maybe if I'd known Mom for a few years before that drunk driver hit her, *I* might be the one with a rebellious streak. Thankfully, I have Daddy and Aunt Rachel.

I can't fathom what would make her human-hating self actually and knowingly bond with one, though. Why? She's not exactly the sharing type, so I'll probably never know the answer.

"That doesn't make what she did any less wrong," I say, laying my head on Quince's shoulder. "She didn't give Brody a choice."

I stare out toward the street, toward the thick green

grass Quince mows every weekend, the cracked sidewalk and the small hibiscus bush trying to consume his mailbox. What I see, though, is the mental image of Doe's well-kissed lips, and me swimming home with Brody. Hopefully by this time tomorrow night the whole thing will be a memory.

"She's not completely lost, you know," Quince finally says. "She's just trying to find her way."

He has tons more sympathy for Doe than I have. He didn't grow up with her. He wasn't the focus of most of her tantrums and pranks. He can't possibly understand.

"She's old enough to know better."

"I know you two have a history," he says. "But I think she wants your respect."

"My respect?" I roll my eyes as far back as humanly—or mermaidly—possible. "She has never done anything to earn my respect."

He faces me, his blue eyes steady. "Maybe she's never thought she had a chance of getting it." His free hand finds mine in the almost-darkness, and he twines his fingers through mine. "Maybe you need to open the door a crack."

I look away. He can't be serious. If Doe ever wanted my respect—and that is a Great Barrier Reef–size if—then she would have shown me respect, too. Instead, she treated me like sea slime.

"It's not that easy," I say.

"You're the princess, Lily," Quince says, his voice low

and gentle. "How should a princess deal with Dosinia?"

I almost say, "I'm not a princess for very much longer," but I don't. Because he's right. Until midnight on my birthday, I *am* the princess. I have a responsibility to my kingdom, to my family, and to Doe to figure out how to get through to her.

If I don't, things will only get worse from here.

With a deep breath that pushes away all the history between me and Doe, I turn and lean toward Quince until our foreheads meet. So close I can feel him breathe.

"How do you always know just what to say?" I ask.

His laugh rumbles through me. "Practice, I guess."

I pull back and give him a quizzical look.

"I spent three years imagining what I would say to you if you were mine," he says, tugging me back close. "I should hope I know what to say now that I've got you."

"Yeah, well, I've had almost eighteen years to practice being the princess," I say, "and I still get it wrong half the time."

"Maybe bigger things take more practice."

"Maybe." But I don't have much more practice time left. This is my final royal duty, and I need to get it right. I just don't know how.

There are digital cameras, sketchpads, and graphite pencils sitting on the art tables when Doe, Shannen, and I walk in after lunch.

Shannen and I exchange a glance and say, at the same time, "Self-portraits."

My shoulders slump. This is my least favorite kind of art project. When we did self-portraits at the beginning of the year, Mrs. Ferraro said we would do them again near the end so we could see how "our perceptions of ourselves" had changed. I've been dreading today ever since.

Mrs. Ferraro is really big on what she calls self-discovery projects—autobiographical collages, representational free-form sculpture, self-portraits. I think it's her personal mission to be both art teacher and therapist.

"Precisely right, Lily and Shannen," Mrs. Ferraro says as we head to our table. "You may begin whenever you're ready. Take a digital photograph of yourself, print it out, and then proceed to sketch your self-portrait."

I sigh as I sling my backpack under our table.

"I'm sure the girls can explain the project to you, Dosinia," Mrs. Ferraro says, before scurrying after the rest of the students trickling in.

"What's to explain?" Doe asks, sliding her briefcase next to her chair. "Click, print, draw."

Doe and I have been on a kind of if-you-don't-bother-me-I-won't-torment-you truce since last night. Saves a lot of tears and bloodshed, but doesn't do much to get the mutual-respect thing going between us. I'm going to have to step up and be the bigger mermaid.

Eventually.

"Pretty much," Shannen says. She grabs the camera. "Who wants to go first?"

"Just get it over with," I say, not in a higher-road mood.

We go out into the hall, where we'll have the cream-colored cinderblock walls as a background. I'm first. Until last night, I probably would have made some kind of over-joyed face for the camera—having found and caught the perfect boy and figured out my future and all, I should be thrilled —but now the best I can manage is annoyed resignation.

Shannen makes a very supermodel pose, with her lips pursed, cheeks sucked in, and eyes smiling as wide as possible. I don't tell her she looks a little crazed. That might influence her sketch.

When Dosinia steps into position against the wall, she asks, "So that's a camera?"

"What?" I twist the camera back toward me, as if needing to inspect it. "Yeah. This is a camera."

"You've never seen one before?" Shannen asks.

Doe shakes her head.

Sometimes it's so easy to forget why she's here—besides to make my life miserable. She knows nothing about the human world and it's my job, my royal duty, to teach her. This is the perfect opportunity to further her human educa-tion. And maybe make inroads on the attitude thing, too.

"Well, then," I say, smiling, "let's do this photo shoot right."

For the next several minutes, Shannen and I coach Doe in a photo shoot of fashion-magazine proportions. At first she just stands there, a blank expression on her face, staring intently at the camera. We give her poses to try, trade out accessories, restyle her hair, until we've exhausted all possible combinations. We even grab a fashion magazine from the classroom to show her what fashion photography really looks like. When Mrs. Ferraro pokes her head out into the hall and says it's time to get sketching, we must have taken over a hundred pictures.

After returning to the classroom, selecting our photos for the project, and printing them out on the computer, we settle in at our table with the paper and pencils.

"That was fun," Doe says quietly, her lower lip chewed between her teeth and her attention on the photo of herself.

"I'm glad," I say just as quietly. "I had fun, too."

Wow. We each said something to the other without breaking out into either a fight or insults. It must be a record. I should declare a Thalassinian holiday to mark the occasion.

Too bad I won't be in a position to declare holidays much longer, because that would have been quite a celebration.

For several minutes, the three of us sketch quietly at our table. I begin by faintly marking the outline of my chin and jaw, my neck, and my hair, giving myself a boundary to work within. Then I move on to smaller features—nose, lips, eyes, freckles. Eyes are always the hardest. I try to keep my pencil extra light so if——when——I have to erase and start over, it won't leave big gouges in the paper.

Mrs. Ferraro comes around to our table for an evaluation.

"Lovely work, as always, Shannen," she says, "though I do wish you would relax your lines. Art is not always crisp. Some of nature's most bounteous beauty is found in rough edges and shadowed contours."

Shannen nods, but I can tell she's mentally rolling her eyes. Mrs. Ferraro has been trying all year to get Shan to loosen up artistically. Clearly it hasn't worked.

I slide my sketch to the left so Mrs. Ferraro can see it better. It's not done or beautiful or perfect or good, even, but I'm not hating it as much as I thought I would. Although I'm definitely better behind the camera than with the pencil, it's not an embarrassing effort.

"Nice, Lily," she says.

Then she moves on.

That's it? No critique or comment or suggestion? Just . . . nice?

For once I'm actually not in hate with my project, and she can't say anything more than "nice"? How disappointing.

I tug my paper back in front of me and hang down over my drawing, pencil clenched in my fist. Whenever we get scathing critiques, Mrs. Ferraro says she wouldn't take the time to tear us apart if she didn't think we had potential. I guess I am potential-less today.

I'm just about to scar my drawing with angry pencil jabs when Mrs. Ferraro, looking over Doe's drawing, says, "Spectacular, Dosinia."

My ears perk up, and although I don't lift my head because I don't want them to know I'm listening, I am intently focused on every word.

"Your use of cross-hatching is extremely evocative for someone who has never taken art before." Mrs. Ferraro holds up the sketch and calls for everyone's attention. "If anyone would like to see an excellent example of impressionist sketching, please come see Dosinia's work."

About half the class comes over and crowds around Doe to study her "excellent example." I try not to heave on my self-portrait.

"Why?" I mutter. "Why does this always happen to me?"

"What?" Shannen asks, drawing the collar of her polo shirt with a—shocking—crisp line.

"Dosinia," I whisper, as if I have to explain. "She always outshines me. Always steals everyone's attention."

"Even Quince's," Doe says casually.

I jerk up to look at her.

I hadn't thought we were talking loud enough for Doe to hear.

Her admirers gone, Doe's focus is back on the sketch below her. But her mouth, her perfectly pouty, overglossed mouth, is pulled into a smirk on one side.

"You do not," I say, my voice low and hard, "have Quince's attention."

Slowly, very slowly, she lifts her gaze from the paper until she's looking at me through her thick mascara-blackened lashes. For half a second she just holds my gaze with a piercing blue stare.

"I will by the time you get back."

My jaw drops open.

Truce over.

We glare at each other across the art table, Doe looking smug and me, I'm sure, looking completely shocked. She cannot possibly be thinking about putting her moves on Quince. Can she?

I'm not worried about Quince. I know he's fully committed to me, and he once told me he likes Doe well enough, but she's too immature for him. He wouldn't be interested in her, even if I weren't in the picture.

That doesn't mean she won't try.

And me having to disappear to Thalassinia for a separation is just the opportunity she needs. The opportunity she wants. The opportunity she—

I gasp.

"You did this on purpose!"

Doe bats her eyes innocently. "Did what?"

Dropping my voice to a furious whisper, I accuse, "You kissed Brody because you *knew* I'd have to go home for the separation. You *planned* this."

Her unfreckled shoulders lift in a lazy shrug.

As she goes back to her sketching, I feel like my blood is on fire. I can't believe she did this. I can't believe she would do something so underhanded, something that would affect Brody's life as completely as the bond does, just to get the chance to steal my boyfriend.

"Is anyone else warm?" Mrs. Ferraro asks. "It suddenly got very balmy in here. Maybe the air conditioning conked out."

On the verge of scratching holes in my self-portrait, I set my pencil carefully down on the table. I take several deep breaths, trying to calm myself and my effect on the moisture in the air around me.

"You've sunk to a new depth, Doe."

She doesn't look up from her sketching.

"When I get back," I say, trying to sound as stern as possible, "you and I are going to have a long talk."

"If you say so."

"I do say so," I reply. "Because if you ever want to get back in the water, you have to go through me. This is not exactly endearing me to your cause."

Though she doesn't look up, her eyes widen a little, as if realizing she hadn't thought this all the way through. But then she dismisses the feeling and goes back to her sketch.

What am I going to do with her? I'm not a problem solver. I'm not good at resolving conflicts or settling disputes, which are just a couple of the reasons I should never be queen, if I were making a list. But with Doe especially I've always been at a loss.

Hopefully Daddy can give me some advice. That'll be one good thing about going home.

6

*B*rody doesn't want to leave his precious Camaro parked at the beach unsupervised, so Quince gives us a ride in his mom's junker car to Seaview Beach Park—the same spot where I first told Quince the truth about me. As impossible as it seems, I think his mom's car is even more of a death trap than his motorcycle.

Dosinia, of course, just *has* to ride along.

"We should be back tonight," I say for, like, the fifteenth time. "Tomorrow morning at the very latest."

That is nonnegotiable. My interview is tomorrow morning. At ten o'clock. If we have to stay the night, I'll still make it as long as we leave first thing. The key to my future and helping my kingdom from land might be in that interview. Nothing will keep me from making the appointment.

Quince pulls out of the driveway and into our street.

106

"Don't go getting any romantic ideas about Benson while you're down there," he says with a smile. "I want you coming back to me."

"Well . . ." I pretend to consider. "He does know how to swim."

Unlike Quince. That was the first of many problems with our bonding. Imagine me, a mermaid, bonded for life with a boy who couldn't even swim. The idea was ridiculous. Now I can't imagine being with anyone else.

"I'm learning," he says.

"You're trying, anyway," I tease.

We've had a couple of lessons, but they have been tough. Whenever we get into the water, I feel a little sad. Even if he becomes an Olympic-class swimmer, like Brody, we both know he will probably never be able to go home with me again. The magical separation Daddy performed—at my request—made sure of that. He's immune to the mermaid bond.

I'm not sure if he senses my sadness. I think he feels that, by learning how to swim, he's getting closer to me. But I can't help worrying that he'll never be quite close enough.

I'm totally fine with my future on land, but still . . . it would be nice to be able to bring him home for a weekend or two. I can't help but hold out a teeny-tiny bit of hope that someday we'll find a way.

I shake off the melancholy thought. No use crying over

something that can't be undone. We're together, and that's all that matters.

"You're right," he says with a laugh. "Couldn't pick a better human to race home with if you tried."

Tugging one of his hands off the steering wheel, I lace our fingers together and squeeze. I know his laugh was forced. As much as he almost always seems to sense what's going on in my head, I'm pretty good at guessing his thoughts, too. Sometimes I think—or hope—that maybe our bond never got fully severed, that we're still magically connected, but I know that's not true. We're just really tuned in to each other. Just how I like it.

The entire time we've been talking, I've been trying to ignore the sounds coming from the backseat. Even if Doe only bonded with Brody to get a window of opportunity with Quince, the selfish sea urchin sure doesn't seem to mind kissing him. Again and again and again.

"When I get back," I say over the smooching sounds, "after my interview in the morning, we can take our ride down the coast."

"I'll have Princess all shined up and ready to go," Quince says as he steers the car into the beachfront parking lot.

We all pile out onto the blacktop and head for the surf line.

While the sand squishes beneath my feet, I focus in on my transfiguration, mentally forming a finkini beneath my shorts. Quince walks with me to the water line, not caring if his biker boots get doused with salt water.

Up the beach a few yards, Doe and Brody are getting in one last makeout session.

As soon as we slip beneath the waves, she'll turn her attention to Quince. I just know it.

"Watch out for Doe," I tell him as I unbutton and peel off my shorts, revealing my finkini of lime green and gold scales.

"I'll take care of her," he says, holding out his hand. "Like she was my own sister."

"No." I give him my shorts and then tug off my flip-flops and set them on top of the shorts. "I mean *watch out for her*. She's devious and has her sights set on you. She set this whole thing up just so she could have time alone with you."

Quince glances at the lip-locked couple. "You're reaching, princess."

"I mean it."

His Caribbean blue eyes look directly into mine. "You have nothing to worry about here."

"I know." I wrap my arms around his neck and tug myself close. "But still . . ."

"Okay." He drops a kiss on my forehead. "I promise." Another on my nose. "I'll watch out for a surprise attack."

And then Doe is completely forgotten as his mouth closes

over mine. His lips have a way of doing that, of making me forget everything else.

"Are you ready to go?" Doe's sharp voice penetrates my kiss-induced fog. "It's only a few hours until sunset."

Well, wasn't that just as transparent as jellyfish in rain? She's eager to get me gone.

I pull back. Reluctantly.

"Yeah," I say. "We should go."

"Go," Quince says, pressing one last kiss to my lips. "I'll be waiting for your call. At your house or mine."

He nods to the pay phone at the edge of the parking lot, which I'm going to use to call him for a ride when Brody and I get back. The coins I need to make the call are tucked into the bra top of my swim tank.

Pulling out of Quince's arms, I turn to Brody. "Come on."

Brody and I head into the surf, leaving Quince and Doe standing on the beach. When we reach the depth where we can go under, I turn back to wave good-bye. And notice that Doe has inched awfully close to Quince's side.

I scowl as I sink beneath the surface, pulling Brody down with me.

I transfigure instantly, shedding my terraped legs for my tail fin. It's somewhat cathartic. The familiar salt water and the magic of my change ease some of the tension Doe's caused. She and her finful of trouble will be waiting when I get back. For now, my focus needs to be on Brody.

Even though we—Doe, Quince, and I—explained the

whole process to Brody last night, I still expect his brain to resist breathing water. To face suffocation rather than risk drowning. To fight, like Quince did, holding on to his last lungful of air with desperate determination.

Instead, by the time I've finished changing into my mer form, Brody is sucking in big gulps of seawater like he was born to it. With Quince, I had to use the strength of my tail fin to hold him underwater until a breath became inevitable. I should have known that Brody the swim star would be the complete opposite.

For three years I dreamed of this moment, imagined it going exactly like this. Brody taking to the mer world as if he'd always been a part of it.

But now that it's here, I only wish it wasn't happening.

"This is awesome," he says, getting even the voice adjustment right on the first try. "I'm totally breathing water."

"Yeah," I say, for some reason annoyed by how easily he's adjusting to the underwater world. "It's Valentine's Day, Halloween, and Christmas, all rolled into one." I turn my back to him and motion for him to grab my waist. He may be fast in the water, but he can't compete with me in mer form. "Let's get swimming."

The feel of Brody's hands on my waist is surprisingly ordinary. No sparks or heat or flashes of light, like when Quince touches me. Which only proves that what Quince and I have is special, and what I'd thought I would have with Brody was nothing but a fantasy. That thought reassures me.

If that whole mess can work itself out, then surely this will, too. Hopefully sooner rather than later.

I take a deep breath and let out all my frustrations about the current situation, because really, Doe's reckless actions aside, I'm happy with how my life is turning out.

With a flick of my fin I push off, sending us out to sea. Out to home.

"Don't forget to stay streamlined," I remind Brody over my shoulder. "And dolphin kick as hard as you can."

"No problem," he says, and instantly my speed nearly doubles.

And as glad as I am that Brody won't slow me down with drag the way Quince did, I can't help but wish there was some way they could trade places right now. Forever.

If wishes were sea horses, then beggars would ride.

Besides, wishing for something impossible is only going to ruin my mood. Again. I should try to make the best of a bad situation. I should be glad for the visit home. I should be glad the situation isn't any more complicated than it already is.

I kick harder, sending us sailing through the water toward Thalassinia. We'll be there before I know it.

With Brody's dolphin kick making up for his extra drag, we make it to the edge of Thalassinia in about half the time it took me and Quince. We sail quickly over the deceptively organic-looking suburbs and industrial sections, heading directly for the royal palace at the center.

I don't even stop long enough for Brody to get a scenic view of the kingdom. I just want this done and behind us. Who knows what kind of havoc Doe is causing at home? Or what kind of moves she's making on Quince?

As we swim up to the palace gates, the twin columns of coral that mark the entrance to the palace grounds, the guards are blocking the path, tugging an object back and forth between them.

"It's mine," Barney says, pulling the object sharply toward him. "I'm the head guard today."

"But I," Cidaris barks back, "am the senior officer." The object jerks in his direction. "I get to hold the scepter."

After watching a few more tug-of-war exchanges, I swim up to them. Daddy is very informal with his staff, so the palace guards are practically family. Especially Cid, who's been in the guard since before Daddy was born. He's like my honorary grandfather.

Even if, on occasion, he acts more like seven than seventy.

"Hi, Cid," I say. "Hi, Barney."

The pair instantly stops their battle, turning to me with giant grins on their faces. Their hands fly to their foreheads in twin salutes of respect. I blush, remembering Brody at my back, and return their salute so they can relax.

"Princess Waterlily!" they exclaim simultaneously.

"We didn't know you were—"

"No one told us—"

"It was kind of a surprise," I say, nodding at my passenger. "For both of us."

Their gazes shift to Brody, who has released my waist and swum to the side so he can get a view of the palace. Then the guards turn their questioning gazes on me. I can read the question in their minds as clearly as if I were telepathic. Anyone could.

What about Master Quince?

"Princess?" Cid asks cautiously.

"Don't worry," I say. The entire palace—the entire kingdom—knows that a couple of weeks ago I decided to return to land to be with Quince. They know, because my decision meant I was also giving up my future as their queen. News that juicy spreads like a red tide.

Returning home with another boy is probably a shock. "This one isn't mine," I say, jerking my thumb at Brody, who is grinning like a fool. He looks like I just handed him the keys to an underwater theme park. "He's Doe's."

"Lady Dosinia?" Barney asks.

Doe's bratty behavior is widely known throughout the palace. They shouldn't be surprised to learn she caused some big-time trouble in her short time on land.

The strangled look on Cid's face suggests I've said something wrong.

"We're just here to get the separation," I explain. "Since Doe's been ex—"

"Here, take the scepter," Cid says, interrupting my explanation and thrusting the forgotten wand into Barney's hand. "Go message bubble the palace that the princess is home."

Barney looks like he wants to argue, but Cid adds, "That's an order, whippersnapper."

After a moment's hesitation, Barney bows to me and then retreats to the guard tower. He doesn't look one bit happy about being sent away.

Cid swims close and lowers his voice. "You should know, Princess, that His Highness has not made Lady Dosinia's situation widely known."

"Oh," I say. "Okay."

"Only his closest advisers and I know of her punishment." He glances at the guard station, as if making sure Barney hasn't emerged. "I think he would prefer that no one else in the kingdom be made aware of the exile."

"Really?" I ask, kind of stunned.

Daddy is usually extremely open about his policies and decisions. Transparency is the key to respect, he always says. So why is he keeping this particular situation a secret?

He must have his reasons. He would never do something like this without careful thought and consideration. Maybe preserving Doe's reputation for future suitors or something? That's fine. I won't be here long enough to have to watch my tongue.

"Is Daddy in his office?" I ask, wanting to get Doe's separation over with and head back to Seaview. "We need to—"

The look of distress on Cid's face freezes me mid-sentence.

"What?" I ask.

"His Highness is away from the palace today," Cid explains as Barney swims out of the tower and back over to our group.

"Away?"

"He's been gone since yesterday," Barney adds. "He went to—"

Cid elbows him in the ribs. "We expect him back in the morning."

The morning? Great. That means I'll be cutting it close on making it back in time for my interview, but I can't start worrying yet. If Daddy's not back first thing tomorrow, then I'll worry.

"Cool," Brody says. "Does that mean I have time to look around?"

His eyes are wide and bright, and he's looking around at all the sea-life-covered structures and underwater gardens with complete and total awe. Thalassinia feels so ordinary to me—it's home—that I forget it's entirely foreign to humans. This whole world of magic and mermaids and under-the-sea is like a shiny new toy for Brody, and I can't exactly begrudge him some exploration. I always knew he was a water soul, born into the wrong world, so of course he's thrilled to be here longer.

With night falling, I can't exactly send him out on his

116

own. I guess I'll have to play tour guide.

"I'll show you around," I say with no enthusiasm. "Just let me go grab a snack from the kitchen." The long swim really works up an appetite.

Cid, who's known me practically since birth and can probably read my mind better than Quince, swims forward and says, "I would be happy to show the young man around, Princess."

"But we're on duty," Barney says petulantly. "We can't just—"

"You're head guard today," Cid replies with a friendly smirk. "You guard. I'll tour."

Barney glares at the scepter clutched in his left hand. "Fine."

I glance at Brody, who looks like he's won the lottery, and then back at Cid. "That would be wonderful. Thank you."

"My pleasure," Cid says.

Then, with Brody swimming after him, Cid heads toward the palace. They haven't gone twenty feet when Brody darts off to follow a school of blue-green queen parrotfish. Cid swims ahead for several seconds—probably giving his favorite speech about the history of the palace—before realizing his ward is gone.

As Cid hurries to catch up, I laugh. "He's going to have his work cut out for him, Barney," I say, trying to make the pouting guard feel better. "Brody is one of the fastest swimmers in the state of Florida."

He looks somewhat pacified. My job here is done.

Since I'm going to be here overnight, I know exactly where to go. When in doubt or cleaning up other people's messes, the best friend's house is always the answer.

7

As I swim up to Peri's house, just outside the palace wall, I bypass the front door and head directly for her window on the top floor. Floating outside her bedroom, I see Peri at her desk, bent over and working intently on a weaving project as her chestnut hair undulates around her. She makes some of the most beautiful cloth the ocean world has ever seen. Her talent is obvious.

This one is made from various shades of green, ranging from the deep mossy tint of codium to the vibrant lime of sea lettuce, with shining strands of gold glittering throughout.

"It's beautiful, Peri," I say, floating into her room. "As always."

"Lily!" she gasps, whipping away from her work and quickly jamming the cloth behind her. "What are you doing here?"

"It's almost funny, really."

In a tragically hilarious way.

I roll my eyes and twist my body into a corkscrew.

I hear some shuffling and then Peri is in front of me, grabbing my shoulders to stop my whirling. Her gray-green eyes look directly into mine. "Is something wrong?" she asks, shaking me slightly. "I thought you weren't coming home until next weekend, just before your birthday celebration."

"I wasn't." I swim over to her collection of designer Oceanista dolls—almost all of them gifts from either me or Daddy—and run my fingers lovingly over their historical costumes and tightly styled hair. "Dosinia happened."

"Dosinia?" she asks, sounding shocked. "What did she do this time?"

"She kissed Brody."

"Brody?" Peri echoes. "*Your* Brody?"

"He's not *my* Brody," I argue. "But, yeah, same boy."

"How did she even meet him?" Peri asks. "Doe hates humans. Why would she go on land?"

Guess Cid wasn't joking about Daddy not telling anyone about Doe's exile, if Peri doesn't know. Her mom is dressmaker to the Thalassinian elite; she hears all the best gossip.

Whatever Daddy's reasons for keeping the whole thing quiet, I still don't hesitate for a second. Peri's my best friend and I tell her absolutely everything. If anyone knows how to keep a secret, it's her.

"This is for your ears only," I say, "but Doe's been exiled."

Peri gasps. "What?"

"Daddy revoked her powers." I swirl away from the dolls and give Peri an oh-joy-for-me look. "He sent her to live with me until she gets past her hate for humans."

"Wow." Peri floats down onto a starfish-shaped cushion in the corner of her room. "She must have messed up drastically. What did she do this time?"

"I don't know." I join her on the next starfish over. "Daddy's always been pretty lenient with her. This must have been over the top, but she won't tell me what she did."

"It must be pretty bad, if even Doe won't own up to it."

Peri sits thoughtfully for a moment, tugging absently at the end a starfish leg. "She really kissed a human?"

I nod.

"Maybe she doesn't hate them any longer."

Ha. Peri has no idea. "Maybe she just hates me more."

I quickly explain my theory about why Doe bonded with Brody, just so I'd have to leave. So she could get her hooks into Quince—not that he'll fall for any of her bait. She could be up there right now, tempting him with fabulous style and flirty laughter. My anger rises just thinking about her.

"Well, that sounds more like her," Peri says.

She's known Doe almost as long as she's known me, so she's not unfamiliar with my cousin's antics. And she's been at enough of Doe's dress fittings that she's also not unfamiliar with my cousin's generally awful attitude. She's seen firsthand the bratty side that Doe tries to hide from the

121

populace beyond the palace walls.

"Anyway, since she can't transfigure, I had to be the one to bring Brody," I say, trying to change the subject off Doe, one of my least favorite topics of conversation. "Only Daddy's away from the palace and won't be back until morning."

"So you're here for the night?" she squeals.

"Looks like."

Not that I'm unhappy to be home. I'd just rather be here under different circumstances, and with a different boy in my wake.

"Excellent!" Peri pushes off her starfish and jets to the door. "I'll get Mom, and we can work on your birthday dress. After a day of fittings with the most horrid sea cows in the kingdom, she'll be thrilled to work on someone normal."

Before I can open my mouth, Peri is out of the room and calling for her mom, whom I love like she was my own. And I can't wait to see what she's whipping up for my dress.

Mrs. Wentletrap made the gown for my sixteenth birthday, a beautiful watercolor print of teals and turquoises, with aquamarine stones sewn into a sparkly starfield along the neckline and the fluttering waves of a seaweed hem. I'd felt every inch the princess that night.

At the time I never would have imagined that two years later, my eighteenth-birthday ball would be my last as Thalassinia's princess.

"Come on," Peri shouts. "We're ready for you in the fitting room."

I can't help the giddy shiver of girlish delight that washes through me.

The Wentletrap fitting room is every little mergirl's dream. The walls are covered in hundreds of fabric samples, all colors, all styles, many decorated with sparkles and pearls and the rarest shells in the ocean. Peri and I tried to count them all once. We gave up when we reached a thousand.

There are accessories, too, drawers full of things that kept me and Peri entertained for hours. Abalone buttons, rainbows of ribbons, beads and sequins and every size of pearl imaginable.

And best of all, in the center of the room there's a gauzy half-circle canopy hanging from the ceiling all the way to the floor, facing an oversized full-length mirror. Perfect for a little mergirl playing dress-up. Or a big mergirl playing dress-up.

"Hi, Mrs. Wentletrap," I say as I swim into the dream room.

"Lily, darling," she says with a smile, pulling me into a welcoming hug. "It's always wonderful to see you. Have you lost weight?"

"Not an ounce," I answer with a laugh. "Do you know how many kinds of pudding they have on land? I couldn't lose weight if I tried."

We all laugh.

It feels good to be in this room, with the two ladies who are practically my second family. It feels . . . normal. No matter what's happening on land, I almost never feel normal. There's that small part of me that will always feel out of place. Sometimes I forget how it feels to belong.

Then, small talk over, Peri's mom turns all business. I'm ushered under the canopy, wrapped in yards of neutral cloth so she can make a model of the gown to use as a pattern without having to risk her beautiful—and expensive—fabrics.

"I'm thinking we can go a little lower with the neckline this time," she says around the straight pins she's holding in the corner of her mouth. This always makes me nervous because I'm afraid she'll swallow one. Even though she insists she hasn't swallowed one in her nearly thirty years as a dressmaker and she's not about to start now.

"You're officially becoming a woman," she continues, thankfully using the last of her pins to secure the fabric around my torso. "We should show off your womanly shape."

My cheeks heat at the subtle compliment.

For the next few minutes, the room is a flurry of pinning and cutting and floating back to evaluate the shape and pinning some more. A sheet of white covers the full-length mirror so I can't see what it looks like in progress. Instead, I focus my attention on Peri. She has always worked with her mom, but today she seems to be more of an equal assistant than just a helper.

And she's obviously been assisting a lot lately.

"Who were you fitting earlier?" I ask, to fill the silence.

"Peri said they were really horrid."

Mrs. Wentletrap throws her daughter a scowl. As if she's one to talk. I've heard more gossip from her than the talkative palace housekeeper, Margarite, could ever hope to know.

Peri ignores the look. "Guess."

"I don't—"

She gives me a come on-you-know-who-I-mean look. Which can only mean one thing.

"Oh, no," I groan. "Not the terrible trio."

"None other."

Now I really feel sorry for Peri and her mom. Astria, Piper, and Venus are three of the worst sea witches ever to swim in the ocean. They're the daughters of nobles and diplomats, so I ran into them a lot growing up, and none of those run-ins ever ended well for me. They never let a chance for a cutting comment float by.

I wouldn't wish their presence on anybody. Those three smile to your face and then harpoon you in the back at the first opportunity. I never thought I'd admit this, but I'd rather spend more time with Doe. At least she's always straightforward in her attitude.

"Sorry," I say, meaning it.

Peri shrugs like it's no big deal. I know that it is. They've always been particularly harsh with her because she's my best friend. Their jealousy is obvious.

I've always defended her, but that only seems to make

them try that much harder to hurt her. If I were queen, I'd have them exiled indefinitely.

"What if the skirt was fitted to about halfway down the fin?" Peri suggests in a blatant change of subject. "And then maybe a short, petticoated ruffle at the bottom."

Both Wentletraps float back a few feet, tilt their heads in unison, and squint at my fin. I know better than to interrupt the thought processing.

"You know what?" her mom says. "I think that might just be the perfect solution."

Peri positively beams at her mom's approval. Since forever she's talked about becoming a lawyer—I think so she could argue cases in my court—but I wonder if she wouldn't be happier following in her mom's wake. Especially since, after the renunciation ceremony on my birthday, I won't ever *have* a court.

"So, Lily," Mrs. Wentletrap says, taking in the skirt to match Peri's idea, "you haven't said what brought you home."

My eyes meet Peri's over her mom's head. Confiding a secret in Peri is easy; she's my best friend. If I *were* becoming queen, I'd make her my adviser in a heartbeat. But her mom is . . . her mom. Like I said, she has gossip issues. Peri gives me an it's-your-call look and a shrug.

I'm not sure why, but I feel compelled to keep Daddy's— and Doe's—secret.

"Just felt a little homesick," I say, which is always true.

"That's completely understandable," she says absently,

still absorbed in her cutting and pinning.

Usually I wouldn't go out of my way to protect Doe, after how awful she's been to me since, oh, forever. But if Daddy thinks it's important for her exile to remain a secret, then I trust his judgment. If she were the type to repay debts, I'd say she owes me for this. Since she's not, I'll just content myself with taking the higher road.

"How long will you be here?" Mrs. Wentletrap asks, floating back to evaluate her work.

"Hopefully just until morning," I say. Then I remember I'm supposed to be here by choice. "I mean, unfortunately only until morning. I have a really important meeting."

Mrs. Wentletrap turns to Peri. "What do you think?

"I think," Peri says, pulling the sheet from the mirror and gesturing for me to take a look, "that it is going to be spectacular."

The vision in the mirror, the girl with silky blond hair, fair freckled skin, and a fin-tight dress that hugs—and accentuates—all the appropriate curves . . . well, she doesn't look like me. She looks like a grown-up with my features, and I definitely don't feel like a grown-up.

With a sigh, I turn away from the mirror. "It's beautiful. Truly."

"Excellent." Mrs. Wentletrap swims to my back and starts pulling out the pins that hold the gown form on my body. "We'll get the dress pieced this week, and as long as you come back for a final fitting before your birthday, it will be as perfect as we can make it."

As they peel the dress off me, I ask, "Have you thought about colors?"

I'm picturing the same water-inspired colors as my sixteenth-birthday gown, only in a more adult shape. Maybe more blue toned, with pale sapphires the color of home. The color of Quince's eyes.

"Of course," she says.

"But," Peri adds, "we're going to surprise you."

My gaze drifts around the room. Just about anything they could choose will be amazing, and I definitely trust their sense of color and fabric. If they told me to wear brown, gray, and orange, I'd say okay. They have never sailed me wrong yet.

"I can't wait."

And I only let myself have a tiny melancholy moment thinking that this will be my last royal gown. Ever.

"I'll be back next weekend," I say to Peri and her mom as I swim out their front door. "I'll come by for the final fitting as soon as I can."

They wave good-bye and I disappear over the palace wall, intent on heading for my room and a good night's sleep in my own bed. I push through the palace doors, hoping to sneak up to my room without drawing the attention of the (frequently oversolicitous) palace staff, and stop short when I see a merman admiring the mosaic in the entry hall.

There is something arresting about his posture.

He is near my age, maybe a year or two older, with cinnamon red hair and a flame-colored tail fin, and wearing a jacket of black and red—the royal colors of Acropora, a kingdom to the southeast of Thalassinia. Though I don't recognize him, there is something extremely familiar about his profile.

He turns my direction, breaks into a grin, and exclaims, "Liliana!"

Liliana? Only one person ever called me that. A boy I haven't seen in ages.

"Tellin?" I ask in disbelief.

"The one and only." He swims the short distance between us and spreads his arms wide, inviting me into a hug.

I kick into his arms. "I can't believe it's you!" I throw my arms around his neck with the enthusiasm of the little mergirl I was when I last saw him. "You're so grown up!"

I swim back to get a good look at my childhood friend. He is so very different from my memory. As a merboy, his hair was a brighter, more flamelike red and his fin was a solid orange. I once heard the terrible trio call him goldfish boy—behind his back, of course, because, after all, he *is* a royal prince.

Not only has his hair deepened into a more flattering shade, but so has the tip of his tail fin, giving the impression that someone dipped him in dark red ink. His body has filled out into that of a young man, and his facial features are a little more chiseled than a nineteen-year-old's should be—a little more drawn in the eyes and beneath the cheeks. He looks like life has been hard on him.

The only thing that hasn't changed is his eyes. They are still the palest blue I've ever seen, kind of like the sky right where it meets the horizon. And they still sparkle with a mischief that drew me into more games of what if than I can remember.

For a time it felt like we played together nearly every day, from morning until night. Then one day, he was gone, disappearing back to his home kingdom. Daddy told me there had been a disagreement with Tellin's father and they wouldn't be returning anytime soon. They never did.

"You're grown up, too," he says with a deep laugh. "It's been more than a decade. You were seven, I think, and I was eight."

"I can't believe it's been that long," I say. "What are you doing here? I thought our fathers weren't speaking."

"They're not," Tellin answers, a worried look settling onto his face. "But my father has fallen ill, and I am acting king for the time being."

"Oh," I say lamely. "I'm sorry to hear that."

I always liked his dad and never understood why the two kings, once the best of friends like their children, had a falling out.

"Then are you here in an official capacity?" I ask.

"Of a sort." He presses a hand to his stomach. "I'm

starved. Does your palace cook still make the best sushi in the west Atlantic?"

"The best in all the seven seas," I boast.

Moments later, we're on stools at the kitchen counter, with palace chef Laver serving up dish after dish of sushi delicacies. This alone is worth coming home for. Even under Dosinia-related circumstances.

"So," Tellin says after swallowing a bite of maguro tamaki, "I hear you've been living on land."

"I have." I study the offerings on the platter and select a Philadelphia roll—I'm a sucker for cream cheese.

Tellin grabs the other Philly roll. "Me, too."

My head shoots up. "Really?"

"Uh-huh," he hums around his mouthful.

"Where?"

"Puerto Rico." He captures a tako nigiri with his sea-sticks. "It's the closest inhabited island to the palace."

Puerrrto Rrrico. The words roll through my mind. I wonder how different human life is in Puerto Rico from in Seaview. It's still tropical, still part of the United States. Still human. Maybe not different at all.

"My Spanish has definitely improved," he says.

"I'll bet."

We spend several minutes devouring the sushi, with Tellin eating two for every one I take—he wasn't joking about being starved—while I ask him about Puerto Rico. Other than a few day trips into Miami for flea-market shopping with Aunt Rachel, I haven't been anywhere on land besides Seaview. I'm curious to know more.

The stories he tells of salsa dancing and scary *caretas* and *cocina criolla* make me want to explore more of the world above the water. Who knows what else I'm missing?

"It's too bad," Tellin says when we've finished off the last of the sushi and waved away Laver's offer for more.

"What's too bad?" I ask when he doesn't explain.

"That our worlds have to remain so separate."

"You mean Seaview and San Juan?"

"No," he says with a sad laugh. "I mean the mer world and the terraped world."

"Oh."

I've wished things were different, too. That wish, that question has definitely come up more than once during my three years on land. Every time I had to lie to Shannen about where I was going for the weekend—thankfully, not an issue anymore since she knows the truth. Every time I had to check over my shoulder ten times before sinking beneath the waves at Seaview Pier, lest some overeager lifeguard try to save me from drowning. Every time Mrs. Ferraro complained about her coffee going cold and I had to fight the urge to say, "Hey, hand it to me. I can warm it up."

Those were the times that made me wonder, Wouldn't it be nice if humans knew? If I didn't have to hide the truth about myself at all costs?

132

As nice as it would be, it's just a dream. A very dangerous dream.

"Yeah," I finally agree, "it's too bad. But also necessary."

Tellin absently swirls his seasticks back and forth over the empty platter.

"Is it?" His eyes have a faraway look. "I don't know."

"Of course it is," I insist. "You know what might happen to us, to all the mer kingdoms. It's just too risky."

He looks up, his eyes sparkling with mischief. "What if?" he asks, starting the game we used to play as guppies. "What if terrapeds knew?"

"Okay," I say, turning to face him. "What if. What if . . . we called a press conference with the kings and queens of all the mer kingdoms?"

"What if," he continues, "our fathers stood side by side to tell the terraped world that merfolk exist?"

The what-if game is kind of like verbal chess, or math proofs. There is a starting point—what if terrapeds knew—and an end goal—the mer and human worlds coexisting. We have to alternate what-ifs to get from the starting point to the goal.

It's not a game with a winner or loser. The journey is the game.

I ponder my next move, full of the fears about what might actually happen if this came to pass. "What if the governments of all the developed human countries sent troops to capture merfolk around the world and lock them away in labs for scientific study?"

Tellin shakes his head. "Out of bounds," he claims, accusing my what-if of going off track. "We're thinking positive."

"Okay," I relent. "What if the governments of all the developed human countries"—I force myself to think positive—"invited the mer kingdoms to join the United Nations?"

"Better." Tellin nods. "What if finfolk around the world walked out of the oceans, rivers, and lakes and shared their knowledge and culture with the terrapeds?"

"What if," I say, imagining this utopian paradise, "humans treated merfolk as equals, rather than mutant creatures?"

"What if . . ." Tellin shakes his head. "Sounds like a dream world to me."

I sigh. "Me too."

"Why don't we do it?" he suggests. "Why *don't* we come out of the ocean?"

I give him a you've-got-to-be-kidding look. "You know why."

"I know it's fear that keeps us trapped in the water," he says, slamming his seasticks down onto the counter. "The fear of what *might* happen. But we don't *know*. It might unfold just as we said."

"That's the dream, Tellin," I say sadly. "But the fear, the thing that *might* happen, that's too terrible to even think about. It's not worth the risk."

"I know." His anger washes away, and he gives me a

glowing smile. "But it's a lovely dream."

"It is," I agree. "A lovely dream."

Unfortunately, the dream can only exist in our what-if game. Too many lives are at stake to reach for the dream and risk facing the nightmare.

$\mathcal{I}$ wake early the next morning to find Daddy sitting on the edge of my bed, gently nudging my shoulder to rouse me from sleep. I blink him into focus before wrapping my arms around him in a fierce hug.

"Good morning, Daddy."

He smiles, making little crinkles around his eyes. "Good morning, daughter."

"How have you been?" I ask, even though I've only been gone a couple weeks.

A distant look starts to drift into his eyes, but he shakes it away. "I have been missing you, of course," he says. "But I understand you have had your fins full with your cousin."

I groan and roll my eyes and make a *tsk*ing sound with my tongue, all at once. "Holy Capheira, yes. You know how she can be."

"I do."

There is an ocean of subtext in that tiny phrase, and I can guess what it's about.

"Why did you send her to me in exile?" I ask. "What did she do? It's not like she hasn't broken rules before." And laws, I add silently, because Daddy might not know about those. I'm taking the high road again. Doe owes me double.

"This was . . ." Again he shakes his head. "I think this is a matter best kept between Dosinia and me."

"Okay."

Daddy has on his king-of-the-seas persona, which means there's no negotiating. Besides, the way everyone is fin-dipping around the issue, I'm starting to think I'd rather not know what Doe did. It might scar me forever.

"Cid tells me you have brought another boy for separation," Daddy says.

"He's not mine," I explain, even though Daddy should know I would never cheat on Quince. "Dosinia kissed him."

Daddy heaves a deep sigh, his chest rising and falling beneath his uniform jacket. "I guess I didn't take away enough of her powers to keep her from getting into trouble."

I've seen that sigh before. Doe lives with our aunt Bells and uncle Portunus in a big manor house at the center of Thalassinia's historic district. But she's spent enough time in the palace that Daddy and I have both experienced plenty of her antics. Like the time she burst into the throne room in a panic, claiming there was a great white on her tail. Or when she hid stinky lobsters beneath the mattress of every bed in the palace—everyone had to sleep in the halls for a week. Or, most famously, the time she convinced the male members of the palace staff that Daddy wanted them to appear shirtless at a royal ceremony involving the heads of several other kingdoms. I was amazed Daddy didn't fillet her alive then.

So hearing that, within her first week on land, she's gotten herself bonded to a human boy is not exactly a shock.

"Meet me in my office," Daddy says, pushing away from my bed. "Bring the boy so we can discuss how to proceed."

I spend a few minutes getting dressed and freshening up before going to find Brody. Margarite, the palace housekeeper, placed him in the South Pacific room—a casual space decorated in black pearls and giant abalone, with wallpaper made from woven sea-palm fronds. It always makes me want to swim to Bora Bora. I've never been, but in my imagination it is as close to paradise as you can get.

I find Brody studying the ceiling of inlaid abalone that almost exactly represents the sky over Thalassinia at dawn. It's a masterpiece—and it's only a ceiling. Even though I grew up here, I'm still in awe of the palace's majesty.

The same awe I see in Brody's wide eyes.

"This place is amazing, Lil," Brody says, echoing my thoughts as we make our way through the palace to Daddy's office. "I can't believe you never told me about this."

"Yeah, well," I say softly, "I'd always planned to."

Thankfully, he misses my double meaning. He doesn't know that for three long years I wanted to bond with him, bring him home to Daddy, and eventually take the throne with him at my side. He also doesn't know that I'm insanely happy that never happened. We are nowhere near as compatible as I always fantasized.

"You know," Brody says, his voice dropping to a serious tone even though he keeps looking excitedly around the hall, "I knew I wasn't good enough for you."

"I—" I choke on my response. He doesn't mean what I think—what I fear—he means, does he? "You—what?"

He stops gawking long enough to face me. He flashes me a heartfelt smile. "I'm glad you connected with Fletcher—he's a great guy."

"He is," I whisper. He didn't come right out and say it, but I definitely get the feeling my secret crush wasn't as secret as I thought. Embarrassment burns onto my cheeks.

"Did you know the roof is covered with *living* sea life?" he asks, turning away, his golden brown eyes wide with excitement as he swims off ahead of me. Even with me in mer form, I have to increase my speed a little to keep up.

I focus on ignoring my sudden humiliation. It's a good thing I didn't find out while I was still crushing on him, because I might have flat out died from mortification.

"Yeah," I answer, making myself pretend that nothing has changed. Apparently Brody is forgetting that I actually grew up here. "Awesome, isn't it?"

By the time we reach Daddy's office, I think my cheeks may have returned to their normal, pale, freckled selves. The royal guards outside the door salute as I approach. I return the salute and briefly wonder how they will greet me when I'm no longer a royal princess. Will they still salute? Or just wave and say hello? Or will they not greet me at all? Will they, like Doe, see me as a traitor, abandoning my kingdom for myself? I can only hope they see I'm trying to make the best choice for both.

They open the doors so Brody and I can enter.

Daddy is at his desk, bent over a stack of papers, studying intently. When his secretary, Mangrove, clears his throat, Daddy finally looks up.

"My apologies," he says, waving us into the seats across from him. "I was just reading over separation law to confirm my suspicions. I'm not called upon to perform separation very often, and I needed to refresh my knowledge."

"Suspicions?" I ask, not liking the sound of that.

Daddy nods gravely. "In order for a separation ritual to work," he says, running his finger along the paper, "both parties need to be present."

"That's dumb." And a definite problem. I think about the missing portion of Doe's mer mark and can come up with only one solution. "Well, you'll just have to lift Doe's exile for a day."

"I'm afraid that is not an option." He doesn't explain

whether it's because he *can't* lift her exile . . . or if he *won't*. The icy edge in his voices tells me not to ask for clarification.

Like I said, I don't want to know.

"Well, then what?" I ask. There's a human boy sitting next to me whose life will permanently change without his permission if the separation is not performed by next weekend's new moon. "It's not like they can stay bonded. They're not in love, and Brody can't become a merman."

"Why not?" Brody asks.

I roll my eyes and ignore him. He doesn't know what he'd be getting himself into. Besides the whole stuck-with-Doe-for-life thing—something I wouldn't wish on my worst enemy, except maybe the terrible trio—there's the whole allergic-to-chlorine thing that would make his swimming career pretty much fatal. Nope, even though Brody obviously loves the water and is enthralled by Thalassinia, I can't let him make that naïve choice.

"There has to be a way," I insist. "I know. You can come to Seaview."

Daddy can't get away often because his duties are pretty much dusk to dawn. But surely he can be gone for just a day. It's a pretty extreme situation.

"That is unnecessary. I have another solution." Daddy turns to another paper in his stack. "An ancient transference of power ritual we located in the royal archives."

"Transference of power?" I lean forward in my seat. "What does that mean?"

"It means," Daddy says, smiling, "that I can temporarily grant you the ability to perform the separation."

Huh. I never even knew that kind of thing was possible.

Daddy gets some of his power from the trident—all the kings and queens of the mer world have them—but a lot of it comes from within him, too. From the power bestowed on him in his ascension ceremony.

I know that if I were bonded right now and being officially crowned on my eighteenth birthday, I would receive some power of my own. I just never knew it could be a temporary thing, too.

But if Doe can't get to Thalassinia and Daddy doesn't want to get to Doe, then I suppose this is the best choice. Plus, it'll be cool to experience the kind of power that makes chilling my morning juice seem like a card trick.

"Okay," I say, bracing my palms on the desk. "Tell me what to do."

Brody and I make it back to Seaview flipper fast, and before I know it I'm standing at the pay phone, waiting for Quince to answer my call. When he doesn't, I hang up, get my coins back, and then dial Aunt Rachel's number.

Before she's even said hello, I hear the chaos in the background.

"Lily?" she asks above the shouting and some squawking and what sounds like drumbeats. "Are you back, dear?"

"What's going on?" I shout.

"Just a little— Stop trying to catch the seagull, Dosinia— you're only frightening the poor thing," Aunt Rachel yells, sounding exasperated. Then, back into the receiver, she says, "I'll tell Quince you're ready."

I start to say thanks, but I hear the click when she hangs up before I even open my mouth.

Joining Brody on the beach, I sink down on the sand and rest my forearms on my knees, mirroring his pose. He seems lost in thought, and soon I am, too. I don't want to think about the chaos that is obviously happening back home—like I said, Doe causing trouble is never surprising. Instead, I keep thinking about Tellin and what if. Would it really be possible for the mer world and the human world to coexist? Without us getting locked away like dolphins in an aquarium?

Maybe we haven't been giving humans enough credit? Maybe it's just movies that make us think that humans will go a little crazy if they discover we're more than myth. If only there were a way to find out.

"I wish I could go back," Brody says.

I angle my head so I can see him from the corner of my eye. He is staring out over the ocean with the kind of longing I've only ever seen in him when he's getting ready to dive into the pool. It's a look that says he's counting the seconds until he's home, until he's in the water again.

"I'm sorry it has to be this way," I say quietly. "Doe just does things without thinking."

I may not know Brody as well as I used to hope, but I know he will dream about his time underwater for the rest of his life. He comes alive in the water, just like I do, so I can imagine how he felt when he could literally breathe it in.

I wish I could make him forget the whole thing, to wipe away the memory so he's not haunted by it, but after giving me the separation powers and explaining the ritual, Daddy warned me against doing a second mindwashing. Twice on the same human can be very dangerous.

Only as a last resort, he said.

So, in other words, unless Brody's about to go on the nightly news.

Still, I wish I could. For his sake.

Brody's lips melt into a wry smile. "I think she knew exactly what she was doing." He forces a laugh. "And so did I."

"What do you mean?"

"I mean——" He shakes his head. "I'm sure this sounds crazy, Lily, but I think she's the one."

"The what?" I choke.

"I don't know how to explain it, exactly. When I'm with Doe . . ." He looks me in the eye. "She feels like home."

And I can tell he means it.

If they weren't separated by half of Seaview or had been bonded longer than a day and a half, I could blame his feelings on the magic, the mystical power that takes two beings and joins them closer than any others. I'd think his mind was muddied by the emotional and physical connection of the bond. But the feeling in his voice, in his eyes, is real.

I know, because I feel the same way about Quince.

"I—" This is definitely a twist I didn't expect. "I didn't know."

"Yeah, well." He shrugs. "I didn't either. Kind of ironic, huh? I spend most of my life acting like a player. I finally find the girl of my dreams *and* being with her means being in the water forever. Everything is perfect, except it has to end before it's even begun."

"I—" Why can't I seem to finish a sentence? I'm just so stunned by the sincerity of his emotion. The Brody I've known, the one I thought I loved for so long, has never been so serious about a girl. Too bad he fell for my squid-brained cousin. "If there were any other way—"

"But there is," he says, turning his body to face me. "You don't have to perform the separation."

"I do." I don't want to break his heart, especially when he's being so open and vulnerable about his feelings, but I have to. "Doe is young and impulsive and doesn't care about anyone but herself." I take a steadying breath, knowing this next statement will hurt. "She only kissed you so she'd be left alone with Quince. She thinks she can steal him away from me."

Brody pushes to his feet. "You're wrong." He dusts the sand off his shorts. "She cares about me, just like I care about her."

"Brody," I begin, not sure how to make him realize the truth about Doe when he's blinded by his feelings. I probably can't, so I try another tact. "There are things you don't know about merkind."

"I don't care."

Oh, he will. "You remember how Doe said I'm allergic to chlorine?" When he shrugs, I continue. "Well, it's more than an allergy. Chlorine is toxic to merfolk. It's fatal—"

"I still don't care."

I jump up to meet him face-to-face. I have to make him understand. "You don't get it," I almost shout. "Your swimming career would be over."

"No, *you* don't get it," he says, shaking his head. "Swimming is just a sport, a means to a college scholarship, at best. Doe is . . ." His face transforms into a sunny grin. "My future."

How am I supposed to argue with that? I feel bad for Brody, I really do. He doesn't win in this situation, either way. I'm trying—in vain—to figure out something to say when I hear the rattle of Quince's mom's car approaching.

"Hurry up," Quince shouts as the car squeals to a stop up the beach from our spot. "I don't know how long your aunt can keep Doe and the seagull apart."

Brody doesn't hesitate, just stalks up the beach and climbs into the backseat, slamming the door shut behind him. I've barely got the passenger door closed before Quince is peeling out of the parking lot and racing for home. We're halfway there by the time I get my seat belt clicked into place, and then we're slamming to a stop at the end of our front walk and Quince is out and running for the door.

When I follow him inside a few seconds later, I'm greeting with a flurry of feathers, a lot of hissing and squawking, and Aunt Rachel, Dosinia, and Quince's shouts.

"Corner it!"

"It's heading for the stairs."

"Stop her!"

"Herd it back into the kitchen."

Brody and I rush toward the noise just in time to see Doe dive for Prithi while Aunt Rachel and Quince wave their arms to keep the wild seagull penned in between the sink and the refrigerator.

Unfortunately, Doe's grab misses Prithi, who snakes between Quince's biker boots and lunges for the bird. The terrified seagull makes a break for the doorway between the kitchen and the hall, which happens to be where Brody and I are standing.

"Duck!" I shout, pushing Brody aside as I leap for the seagull. It flies right between my hands and, just when I think it's going to escape, I tighten my grip and feel the weight of its body between my palms.

"Got it!"

"Thank heavens," Aunt Rachel gasps.

Quince, who turned his attention to Prithi when the gull escaped, says, "And I've got the cat."

Not that Prithi is pleased to have been caught by a human when there's a bird and two mermaids in the room. But at least the chaos is contained.

"Is this a messenger gull?" I ask, tucking the bird close to my body.

"No," Aunt Rachel says with a stern look at Doe. "It's a seagull."

"I'm sorry, all right?" Doe says, not sounding sorry in the least. "I didn't know there were non–messenger seagulls. They don't exactly hang out in Thalassinia."

"Doe," I sigh.

"I thought maybe Brody had sent me a message," she argues. Her voice is tight, and I get the feeling she's on the verge of tears.

But I know better than to show her sympathy. If there is one thing Doe cannot stand, it's embarrassment. She tends to process the emotion poorly and turn it against others, in the most cool and calculating ways possible.

"We understand, dear," Aunt Rachel says, way more accepting than me, as always. "It will take you a while to adjust to life on land."

"Life on land? There is no *life* on land," Doe shouts, and we all jerk back at her sudden outburst. Her reactions are usually far more controlled, far more cutting than explosive. "I don't want to adjust, I don't want to be on land. I *hate* being stuck here."

I'm stunned into shock.

Not by her statement, because I know how she feels about land. But Doe is almost always in control, never betrays any true emotions or feelings stronger than mild annoyance. No one has ever gotten this kind of raw reaction from her, not even when Kitt and Nevis cut off all her hair when she was eleven.

Maybe it's her land temper. Most merfolk spend at least some time on land, and that teaches them how to control their runaway emotions to some degree. Since her parents died, Doe hasn't set foot on land for more than a few minutes at a time—and then only to get to the next body of water. When she visited me and Quince on Isla Amorata for our couples-counseling challenge, I was shocked that she stayed on the island for a couple of hours.

Her hormones must be going crazy after a whole week.

Her eyes are wide and a little wild. I've never her seen her quite so out of control. I have a bad feeling that things are about to go very wrong.

"I just want to go home," she screams. "I don't want to be surrounded by you horrible humans anymore."

"Horrible humans?" Brody breaks the silence. "Is that what you really think?"

To her credit, Doe only blinks once before answering. The control is back in place. Everything about her—her voice, her demeanor, her eyes—is icy cold as she says, "Yes." She takes a deep breath, and her chest is shaking. "I hate all humans. They're vile, selfish, dangerous creatures who don't deserve to live when my parents are dead." She looks Brody right in the eyes as she says, "I wish Uncle Whelk hadn't stopped me."

After Brody's beachfront confession, this must feel like a swordfish to the heart. I tried to tell him what Doe is really like, but I can't take any joy in this particular I-told-you-so.

The tension between Doe and Brody chills the room. If Doe had her powers, I'd think she'd chilled the moisture in the air. In this case, though, her frigid emotion is enough to do the job.

I think Aunt Rachel, Quince, and I all sense that this does not involve us, because we all remain frozen and silent.

I knew Doe hated humans—no one who grew up with her could know otherwise—but not like this. Not enough to wish them harm. That bad feeling I had earlier? Well, it's back, times a thousand. Because if Doe has this kind of pure hatred inside her, I can only imagine that it has something to do with her exile. Something very, very bad.

In the end, it's Brody who poses the question we've probably all been thinking. It's Brody who counters her emotion with flat, emotionless words.

"Why did you get exiled?" he asks coolly. "What did the king stop you from doing?"

Doe is like a statue. Arms rigidly at her sides, breathing shallow, back stiff. The only sign that she is alive is her mouth moving as she says, "I stole the king's trident."

I gasp, shaking my head as if I can ward off the statement

I sense is coming next. Daddy's trident is one of the most powerful magical instruments in the seven seas. In the hands of someone full of burning rage and hate . . . Tears sting at my eyes.

"And I tried to wipe out the East Coast with a tsunami."

"Oh, dear," Aunt Rachel gasps.

Quince, still clutching Prithi in his arms, says, "Damn."

Brody doesn't say a word. Doesn't betray any reaction at all, as if Doe had said she tried to send us a rain of hibiscus blossoms. Then again, what kind of reaction should a boy have when he learns that the girl he loves tried to kill him and all of his kind? That's the kind of situation that pretty much defies reaction.

Robotically, his movements jerky, he turns to leave.

"Brody," Doe cries, her ice cracking.

But he doesn't look back.

A few seconds later the sound of the screen door clanging shut echoes through the house. Quince catches my attention across the kitchen and lifts his brows in question.

I open my mouth, wanting to say something, but no words come out. In the end I just shake my head. This is beyond my comprehension. I knew Doe was a brat and that she hated humans, but I never would have guessed that she was this malicious. To think of all the lives . . .

The tears spill from my eyes, and I can't bring myself to imagine the devastation.

"Let me take the gull," Aunt Rachel says, her voice

shaking with carefully contained emotion as she crosses to me. I hand over the bird, and Aunt Rachel disappears into the living room, presumably to send the gull out the front door.

Also, I'm sure, to get as far from Doe as possible.

Several long moments pass before I recover my ability to speak.

"Do you know," I begin, "what kind of destruction you might have caused?"

I picture all the humans who might have been swept away in the tsunami. Quince, Shannen, Brody, and Aunt Rachel, and countless others. Tellin and I and other merfolk living on land might have survived, but only if we avoided the debris wall that would plow over the land like a bulldozer. I never knew she held that much hate in her heart.

Doe shrugs, recovering her unaffected attitude, as if it's no big deal. A facade. I'm not a violent girl, but I've never wanted to slap anyone more.

"Uncle Whelk would never have let that happen," she replies. Only the quiver of her lower lip betrays her awareness of the situation. The gravity of what she almost did. "He stopped the wave before it got half a mile from Thalassinia."

"And that makes it okay?" I demand, crossing to her and standing toe to toe. "What if he hadn't been able to stop it? What if—"

I can't finish the thought. It's too terrible.

"He did," Doe spits. "I don't see what the big deal——"

"You don't see?"

If Quince hadn't dropped Prithi and thrown himself between me and my cousin at just that moment, I think I might have strangled her.

"Lily," he says, sounding all calm and not nearly as homicidal as I feel. Doesn't he know that he and his mom would have been counted among the victims? "This isn't going to solve the problem."

"It might," I snarl.

"No." He cups my chin and makes me look him in the eyes. "You know it won't. Your father sent her to you because he thinks you can help her get past this. He wants you to heal her. It's your duty."

I slump. Duty. The one word that can change everything. All the anger and terror and fire ebb away, because I know Quince is right. Yelling at Doe is not the solution. There's enough hate in the room already.

"I don't know what to do," I whisper so only Quince can hear. "How do I fix her?"

I can't change the past. I can't go back in time and stop the deep-sea fishing boat that caught her parents in a dragnet, shredding their fins and trapping them until a great white came along. The kingdom was in mourning for months. Clearly, Doe blames the entire human race, and all that pain and resentment has been boiling inside her for years.

How can I make her forgive humankind? And re

not all of them show such disregard for life?

"It will take time," he says. "She needs to lea

and, eventually, love humans. It will take only

glances over my shoulder, toward the living room

Aunt Rachel."

An image flashes in my mind, of Brody sittin

me on the beach, telling me he thought Doe was

"Maybe not Aunt Rachel."

Sure, Brody is furious at Doe right now. So a

we all, I think. But the kind of feelings he confe

just disappear because of one incident, especial

happened before they even met. From her reac

Brody walked out, I don't think Doe is as indiffer

as she'd like us to believe. There is strong emotio

her part, too.

Brody will come back around. Eventually. An

feelings, his love, will transform Doe.

It's the only way I can imagine.

I nod at Quince, silently telling him that n

worn off and he doesn't need to protect Doe a

steps aside and I walk up to her.

"I don't know if I will ever forgive you for wh

I say quietly, "but I'll try. And I'll also try to te

most humans are kind, well-meaning, and wil

others in need. If they had known your parents w

154

"He did," Doe spits. "I don't see what the big deal—"

"You don't see?"

If Quince hadn't dropped Prithi and thrown himself between me and my cousin at just that moment, I think I might have strangled her.

"Lily," he says, sounding all calm and not nearly as homicidal as I feel. Doesn't he know that he and his mom would have been counted among the victims? "This isn't going to solve the problem."

"It might," I snarl.

"No." He cups my chin and makes me look him in the eyes. "You know it won't. Your father sent her to you because he thinks you can help her get past this. He wants you to heal her. It's your duty."

I slump. Duty. The one word that can change everything. All the anger and terror and fire ebb away, because I know Quince is right. Yelling at Doe is not the solution. There's enough hate in the room already.

"I don't know what to do," I whisper so only Quince can hear. "How do I fix her?"

I can't change the past. I can't go back in time and stop the deep-sea fishing boat that caught her parents in a dragnet, shredding their fins and trapping them until a great white came along. The kingdom was in mourning for months. Clearly, Doe blames the entire human race, and all that pain and resentment has been boiling inside her for years.

How can I make her forgive humankind? And realize that not all of them show such disregard for life?

"It will take time," he says. "She needs to learn to like and, eventually, love humans. It will take only one." He glances over my shoulder, toward the living room. "Maybe Aunt Rachel."

An image flashes in my mind, of Brody sitting next to me on the beach, telling me he thought Doc was his future. "Maybe not Aunt Rachel."

Sure, Brody is furious at Doe right now. So am I. So are we all, I think. But the kind of feelings he confessed don't just disappear because of one incident, especially one that happened before they even met. From her reaction when Brody walked out, I don't think Doe is as indifferent to him as she'd like us to believe. There is strong emotion there on her part, too.

Brody will come back around. Eventually. And maybe his feelings, his love, will transform Doe.

It's the only way I can imagine.

I nod at Quince, silently telling him that my fury has worn off and he doesn't need to protect Doe anymore. He steps aside and I walk up to her.

"I don't know if I will ever forgive you for what you did," I say quietly, "but I'll try. And I'll also try to teach you that most humans are kind, well-meaning, and willing to help others in need. If they had known your parents were trapped at the bottom of the ocean," I say, not stopping when she jerks back at the mention of her parents, "they would have done whatever it took to save them."

She shakes her head as if she doesn't believe me. That's fine. I already knew she was going to take convincing. These are things I can't just *tell* her, I have to *show* her. *Brody* has to show her.

"As much as I want to send you to the opposite side of the world right now," I say, needing her to know how much this hurt, "I'm going to help you instead."

"How?" she asks, and I can almost believe that she *wants* me to succeed.

I can almost believe her eyes are glowing with a sheen of tears.

In that instant I realize what I need to do. There is only one way to ensure that Brody forgives her and that she gives him the chance to prove all her past feelings wrong. I just hope they both forgive me in the end.

"The only way I know how," I answer. Closing my eyes, I say, "I'm going to leave you bonded to Brody."

My eyes blink open at her gasp.

Beneath the hatred and the aloofness and the frigid protection of her emotions, I see something new in her piercing blue eyes. Maybe I notice it only because it's what I'm looking for, but I almost think I see a spark of . . . hope.

And that spark gives me all the reassurance I need to

believe that Doe can be healed. It just has to happen before her bond with Brody becomes permanent. I could never leave him bonded to someone who hates what he is. That would be too cruel. For them both.

For now, though, it's our only chance.

9

*B*rody doesn't show to pick Doe up before school Monday morning—not that I expected him to. Neither did she, apparently, since she locks herself in the bathroom and insists she's too sick to go. But I know the truth—she's not sick, she's heartbroken.

While a good cousin might show sympathy and commiseration, I'm actually thrilled. Because this means Doe cares about Brody. A lot.

I don't argue about her feigned illness because her staying home gives me a chance to talk to Brody first. After two mostly sleepless nights, alternately imagining what might have happened if Doe's tsunami had succeeded in reaching Seaview and formulating what I need to say to convince Brody to help, I'm exhausted and ready to face him. This won't be easy.

There is no news-team footage to review in the studio,

so I stake out his economics classroom instead. I'm watching the halls intently, so I see him a while before he sees me. Which means I see him notice me, jerk back, and then, after a brief mental debate, decide to ignore me. He tries to walk right past me into the classroom, but I throw out my arm and block the doorway.

He stops but doesn't look at me. "What?"

"We need to talk," I say. Hurt and pain are practically radiating off him. Not that I blame him, of course. We just don't have another choice. "It's important."

"No thanks." He tries to push past me, but I steel my arm and hold him back. I allow myself half a second to be pleased with my own strength.

Then it's back to work.

"Please." I'm not above begging. This is way more important than my pride. I have to make him see that this is about more than just him and Doe. "Just give me five minutes."

"Fine." He finally looks at me. Then his watch. "Five minutes. Go."

I tug him a little way down the row of lockers, out of earshot of the classroom full of students, before I begin. "I know what Doe did was unforgivable."

I take his snort as an agreement.

"I'm not asking you to forgive her." Yet. "I'm so mad myself I could boil water. But you have to understand her history." I give him a quick rundown of her parents' death, a story that could elicit sympathy from a beluga whale, and am relieved when I see his rigid stance relax a little. Progress. "Clearly, none of the therapists she's seen have helped. She's still consumed by the past. By her emotions. She's been living with this rage for years." I duck down and to the right to catch Brody's gaze. "My father sent her here to learn that her misconceptions—her clearly *dangerous* misconceptions—are wrong."

"So what?" Brody's eyes roll away from mine, like he can escape the topic of conversation if he avoids eye contact. "What does that have to do with me?"

"Well," I begin, uncertain but hopeful, "I know you have feelings for her."

His gaze swings back to mine. "Not anymore."

I expected this; am ready for it even. He's hurt and confused and just reacting—which, not so coincidentally, is exactly what Doe is going through. If I can just push through emotion and get to the (hopefully) rational Brody inside, then I have a chance.

"I don't think that's true," I insist, crossing mental fingers that I'm reading the situation right. "You said you thought she was the one. Your future. Feelings like that don't just vanish."

He shrugs, which is at least better than an outright denial. In all honestly, I'm not entirely sure I believe that. I mean, look at what happened to my feelings for Brody. Three years of absolute, undying, *one-sided* love, gone. In a heartbeat.

But that was different. I discovered what love was really

like, and that made what I felt for Brody seem as shallow as a tide pool.

But Brody can't call his feelings for Doe shallow any more than I can call my feelings for Quince the same. I saw the emotion in Brody's eyes, I felt it, and I know it's for real. Just as I saw the emotion in Doe's eyes when he walked out last night.

That's my main selling point.

"And I think—I mean, I hope . . ." I take a breath. "Doe has feelings for you, too."

Brody's gaze sharpens, his brows scowl low, as if not sure whether he should dare to hope there is truth in what I said. I'm daring to hope, so he can too.

"I think we can use your feelings for each other," I explain, "to show Doe that humans and merfolk are not so different as she believes. If she loves you—"

Brody's laughter cuts me off.

"Right," he snarks. "She hates what I am. Not *who* I am, but *what* I am. Something I couldn't change even if I wanted to. How could she possibly love me?"

"Because love doesn't care about prejudices," I say. This is something with which I have firsthand experience. "Just look at me and Quince. I thought I hated him for three years." I don't add the part about where I thought I loved Brody. "True love didn't care what I thought, and it won't care what Doe thinks."

160

Brody clenches his jaw and works his lips, like he's considering my argument. I slip my hands behind my back, beneath my backpack, and cross my fingers as tightly as I can. If I weren't wearing flip-flops, I'd be crossing my toes, too. This situation needs as much good luck as it can get.

Finally he relaxes and asks, "What do you want me to do?"

Sweet angelfish! My entire body explodes with relief. I didn't realize until this instant just how tense I was about the outcome of this conversation.

"Give her a chance," I answer, trying to keep my overjoyed smile from spreading across my lips. "Talk to her. Spend time with her. Make her fall so in love with you, she forgets you're a human." I lay a reassuring hand on his shoulder. "That's all it will take."

I hope.

His gaze drifts to the ceiling, like he'll find the right answer written on the dingy acoustic tiles. I've never seen Brody so thoughtful and serious before. This gives me even more hope that my plan will work. Doe's already worked some positive changes in Brody. It's only a matter of time until he works some in her.

"Okay." Brody nods, not looking at me. "I'll try."

He turns and heads into his class. I take off for American Government, hoping that everything I just told Brody is true.

"Maladroit."

"Um . . ." I search my brain for the definition, knowing we've studied this one at least twice. Finally, just as I'm about to give up, it comes to me. "Clumsy."

That should be an easy one for me since I *am* maladroit. At least on land.

One of Shannen's study techniques is to visualize an image that exemplifies the vocab word. I picture myself wearing a T-shirt that says MALADROIT—I hope it doesn't matter if it's spelled wrong—and then tripping over my own flip-flops into a giant bowl of today's side dish, saffron rice.

"Excellent," Shannen says. She flips through the stack of flash cards in her hands, chooses one, and reads, "Pretentious."

While I search for this definition, Shannen spoons a bite of yellow rice into her mouth and Quince flips through a motorcycle magazine. With the SATs coming up this weekend, I'm trying to cram in as much last-minute studying as possible.

Shannen has already taken—and, of course, aced—the test.

Quince, on the other hand, has no intention of taking it. He already has a job lined up with a construction company, thanks to his current job at the lumberyard. With his brain and skills, I think he'll be foreman within a year.

If only my future were that easy.

"Lily," Shannen prods, waving the definition flash card before my eyes. "Pretentious?"

Without thinking, I blurt, "Pompous. Arrogant."

"Awesome!" Shannen cheers.

This mental image pops into my mind without any effort. The terrible trio. I can't imagine anyone more pompous or arrogant than Astria, Piper, and Venus. Of course, several other vocabulary words apply equally. Vindictive. Malicious. Haughty.

In my mind, the words transform into giant foam letters and start bonking the terrible trio on their heads. I suppress a giggle.

When Shannen starts digging through the stack again, I beg, "Please. No more. My brain can't take it."

She shrugs, as if it's my funeral if I don't cram in ten more vocab words at lunch, but doesn't argue the point. Honestly, I think my brain is completely full. I couldn't handle another piece of information, and I just hope the ones I already have don't start falling out before Saturday.

Coming to my aid—as all good boyfriends should—Quince asks, "Doe called in sick today?"

"Yeah," I say. "I think it was for the best. Gave me a chance to talk to Brody first."

"Why?" Shannen asks. "What happened?"

I hesitate, not sure if Shannen should know what Doe did. I'm not sure *anyone* should know what she did. I wish I didn't.

163

Now I totally understand why Daddy kept her exile—and the reason for it—a secret. She's a dumb kid with a big grudge, but some people wouldn't be able to see that she was acting out from a place of pain. I didn't, at first. Others might hold it against her forever. If I can help her overcome her issues, then it's better if they don't know about her big mistake.

So, even though I hate lying to my best human friend—to anyone, really—I say, "She and Brody had a fight. I'm trying to help them patch it up."

"Why?" she asks. "I thought you wanted to keep them apart."

See, lies always lead to more lies and more complications.

"I've had a change of heart," I admit. "Realized they might actually be good for each other."

Shannen shrugs. "If you say so."

I exchange a glance with Quince. He nods. I think we both know this is the only option—keeping Shannen in the dark, trying to encourage Doe's feelings for Brody. It's the only possible way for everything to end up right in the end.

Shannen pulls another set of flash cards from her backpack. Sliding one across the table to me, she says, "Solve for x."

I groan. Math is . . . not my strong suit. Then again, when it comes to the SATs, I don't think I *have* a strong suit. I dutifully pull out a pencil and prepare to spend the rest of lunch trying to beat the equation into submission. Then I sense a presence at my side.

"Lily?"

I turn to smile, relieved to be saved from math by Miss Molina. Then I see the concerned look on her face. The disappointment.

Son of a swordfish! The interview. In all the craziness when I got back from Seaview, I completely blanked on the interview with Miss Molina's friend at Seaview Community.

"Oh, no!" I gasp. "I'm so sorry. I completely forgot. I'm so, so sorry. There was this whole . . ." I struggle to find the words to describe what happened without really describing what happened. Where are my vocab words when I need them? "Crisis!" I finally blurt. "My cousin got sick and it was really bad. I—" The look in her eyes, like I've failed her bigtime, is killing me. "I should have called or something. I'm just . . . I'm really sorry."

"I don't know what to say." She looks at me like she doesn't even know me. "I didn't remember you to being so irresponsible."

"I'm not," I exclaim. "I mean, I was. This weekend. But I'm usually not at all."

She takes a deep breath, like she's trying to decide what to do about me. I silently will her to give me another chance. Maybe she doesn't buy my sick-cousin story, but if I could tell her the truth, she would totally understand.

Times like this are when I really wish Tellin's what-if could come true. Not that I would relish telling a teacher that one of my relatives tried to wipe her and the entire East Coast off the map. It would be a better explanation than the one I've got, though.

"Since this was so uncharacteristic," she says.

I suck in a hopeful breath.

"I told Denise there must have been an emergency." She schools her features into a very stern look. "She has graciously agreed to reschedule for next Saturday."

"Great. I can—"

Shannen clears her throat and nods at the flash cards.

"Oh. Oh, no." I give Miss Molina what I imagine is a pained look. "The SATs are on Saturday. I'll be there all morning."

She gives me a reassuring smile. "I know. Your appointment is at five."

"You're awesome," I say, meaning it. "I won't let you down again."

"I know you won't." But as she walks away, I think I hear her mutter, "At least I hope you won't."

"You." I point at Shannen. Then at Quince. "And you. Make sure I don't miss this meeting. It could mean my entire future."

"Got it," Quince says before returning his attention to the magazine.

Shannen pulls out her cell phone—a huge no-no on campus, but I guess this qualifies as an emergency—and starts punching buttons. "I've sent myself an email reminder."

I relax a bit.

Nothing can keep me from making the appointment this time.

"Now," Shannen says, waggling the flash card on the table, "solve for x."

I groan, but it's halfhearted. After the freakout about missing my meeting, a little math equation seems like an easy task.

$\mathcal{T}$he first thing Quince and I hear as we push through the kitchen door is Doe laughing. Maybe she's sneaking television online again. I caught her watching an *I Love Lucy* marathon last week, although she pretended that she just didn't know how to work the mouse.

Then I hear another voice. A male voice. A non-Brody male voice.

"She'd better not," I mutter as we head into the living room.

But when we get there, I'm shocked frozen at the sight before me. Doe is sitting on the arm of the corduroy armchair, feet on the coffee table, and the male in question is sitting on the floral sofa. The shock of cinnamon red hair identifies him immediately.

"Tellin!" I blurt.

He stands and faces me, arms wide for a hug. "Liliana."

168

"I didn't know you were coming for a visit," I say, jumping into his hug.

"Nor did I," he says, "until I found myself swimming ashore in Seaview."

A loud throat clearing from behind reminds me of my manners. I pull out of Tellin's hug and grab Quince's hand, tugging him forward. "Tellin, this is my boyfriend, Quince."

Tellin gives him that male nod that girls can never quite replicate exactly.

"Quince," I say, beaming at him, "this is Tellin. One of my closest guppyhood friends and crown prince of Acropora."

They shake hands, and I get the feeling there's a little battle of grips before they separate. Tellin has filled out a lot since we used to play together, but my money is still on Quince. Though his arms are hidden by the sleeves of his leather jacket, I can imagine his biceps flexing nicely in the up-and-down movement

"Pleased to meet you," Tellin says, shaking me out of my reverie. "Lily told me much about you last weekend."

"Funny." Quince throws me a questioning glance. "She didn't mention you at all."

Down, boy. I lean closer into his side to reassure him that there's nothing to worry about. Tellin is an old friend, nothing more.

"I forgot," I explain. "If you'll recall, we found a bit of a crisis in motion when we got home."

Quince crosses his arms over his chest, not appeased by my excuse.

He definitely has a bit of a jealous streak in him, but for the most part he keeps it under wraps. It's stopped peeking out around Brody, but I guess strange boys showing up in my living room bring it back to the surface.

"Tellin's practically my brother," I say, to clarify.

Quince nods, showing he trusts me. "I need to get to work. I'll stop by after."

Then he leans down to kiss me, just like that time in the library. Hand behind my neck, full lips soft and warm on mine. When he sees what must be a completely dazed look in my eyes, he winks. And then, with a wave good-bye to Doe and Tellin, he's out the front door.

When we three merfolk are alone, I ask, "This wasn't just a coincidental visit, was it?"

Doe's eyes widen innocently.

Tellin just smiles. "No," he agrees. "It was not."

"Then why don't we take this into the kitchen," I suggest, "so we can talk over a plate of Aunt Rachel's white-chocolate macadamia-nut cookies?"

"Count me out," Doe says, heading for the stairs in what almost seems like a desperate retreat. "I need another bath."

She's gone before I can reply.

Like she can't wait to get away from me.

Whatever. I'm not the cause of her problems—I'm trying to help solve them.

"Guess it's just the two of us then," I say to Tellin with a smile. "More cookies for me."

I wave him into a chair at the dining table while I arrange a nice stack of cookies on a plate. I pour us each a glass of milk and then take the trayful to the table. I've consumed two milk-soaked cookies before I feel ready to talk.

"So," I begin, "why are you in Seaview?"

He swallows the last of his third cookie. "What if."

"What if." I sigh. This is what I'm afraid of.

"I can't stop thinking about it, Lily," he says, sliding from his chair across the table to the one next to me. "Since our conversation in Thalassinia I'm consumed with the idea of our what-if."

I've been thinking about it too. Especially considering what's going on with Doe. The thought has crossed my mind that, if the mer world weren't a secret, precautions might have been in place and Doe's parents might never have died. Things would be so different right now.

Sadly, the other risks and losses far outweigh that potential gain.

He gets up and starts pacing. I've never seen Tellin in terraped form, and I wonder briefly what his legs look like under his pants.

"I'm tired of hiding in the ocean." He stops behind a chair and grabs the back with both hands. "I want to tell the world—the whole world—who and what I am."

"You know that's not possible," I argue, even if I wish

171

it were. "It's not responsible. Think of how many merfolk would be put at risk."

"That's melodramatic," he returns. "There will be a period of adjustment, to be sure, but I believe that terrapeds and merfolk can coexist peacefully."

I shake my head slowly, sadly. "I don't—"

"I think you believe it too." He drops back into the chair and lays his hand over mine. "You wouldn't be living on land if you didn't."

"I . . ." The idea is too big; my mind is swimming. "Even if I did," I insist, "there's nothing we could do about it. The heads of all the mer states would have to agree. We can't force them to take that kind of risk."

"I know it can't happen overnight," he says. "But you are the royal princess of Thalassinia, and I'm the crown prince and acting king of Acropora. With our joined forces, we can initiate the tides of change."

Could we? I wonder. If Tellin and I were to put the resources of both our kingdoms to the effort of trying to bring the mer world to a consensus about revealing ourselves to the human world, could it happen?

Should it happen?

Even if it *might* be possible, we'll never find out.

"I'll admit it's a brilliant dream," I say. "But you're forgetting one thing."

He lifts his cinnamon brows, waiting.

"After my birthday next Tuesday, I will no longer be a

royal princess. As an unbonded heir, at midnight I will sign away my title."

Tears prickle my eyes at the thought. I've been a princess all my life, raised to be the future queen and to accept all the responsibilities my position entails. To behave with decorum and compassion and with the greater good in mind. The idea that, with one scrawl of my name, all that will be gone . . . well, it makes a mergirl sad.

Not that I would change my decision. I would never be a great queen, and Thalassinia deserves a great queen. I belong with Quince—I belong on land. Which makes Tellin's what-if all the more appealing.

Living on land means living a lie. The possibility of discarding that lie, of admitting my true identity, of helping my kingdom openly from land, is an enticing prospect.

It's also an unattainable dream.

"It doesn't have to be this way, Lily."

"Yes," I say, my throat tight with tears. "It does. I'm renouncing my title and living on land as a practically human girl. It's the choice I've made."

"But what if you didn't have to choose?" He lifts my chin until he can look me straight in the eye. "What if I offered a solution that would allow you to remain with your beloved *and* fulfill your duty to your kingdom?"

Love and duty. If only. My heart beats faster. "What solution?"

His pale blue eyes don't blink. "Bond with me."

"What?" I bark with a strangled laugh. "That's ridiculous."

"Is it?"

Of course it is. I love Quince, and Quince loves me. I'm not about to go bonding with another boy, just because he happens to be a mer prince with some big ideas—even if they are big ideas I happen to agree with.

"I don't mean a true bonding," he explains. "A bond in name only. So you could remain Thalassinia's princess—her crown princess, and her future queen."

"That's . . . I don't know," I say, processing out loud. "I can't bond with you. You're like my brother."

"Think about it, Lily." He leans closer. "One brief kiss, and everything remains as it should be."

He makes it sound so easy.

One little kiss.

Could I do it? Could I kiss Tellin to retain my title? It may seem simple, but I have a feeling it's way more complicated than that. There's bond magic and hurt feelings and jealousy and a whole ocean of other obstacles that make this a very bad idea.

Besides, what's in it for Tellin?

"Why?" I ask. "Why would you want to do this? Sacrifice your future happiness with a mermate to bond with me, when you know I could never love you?"

"For the greater good," he says, his spine straightening. He looks every inch the prince, the king, even. My young friend is long gone. "You understand the demands of royal duty. The mer world needs progressive leaders who can take us into the future. Who can help our world become far more than we have been in the past." His eyes soften. "You know I love your father as my own, but he is mired in the old ways. Thalassinia needs you and your experience on land and your commitment to the ocean environment. It is your *duty* to lead them."

This is all so overwhelming—the idea that I might be able to retain my title, I might still be able to accept my responsibility as Thalassinia's queen, all while remaining true to Quince.

But *would* I be true to Quince? I'm sure he would understand the need for the single kiss—or at least he'd pretend to understand—but the bond is never that cut-and-dried. As he and I learned a few weeks ago, the bond plays with your emotions and your thoughts, magnifying whatever feelings already exist. Bonding with Tellin wouldn't be as simple as kiss-and-move-on. We would be connected for life, for a century or more.

I can't take the risk that this sham bond might eventually come between me and Quince.

Looking into Tellin's expectant gaze, I shake my head. "I'm sorry." If he had ever been in love, he would understand. "I just . . . can't."

"You mean you won't."

"Yes. Both." I give him a sad smile. "We each deserve

better than that kind of empty connection. And Thalassinia deserves better than me."

The muscles in his neck tense, and he looks so wound up that I want to rest my hand against his cheek to tell him everything will be okay. But who am I to know whether everything will be okay? I'm just struggling to get through the day-to-day.

"I'm not giving up," he finally says. "I have until next Tuesday at midnight to convince you of the merits of my proposal. You will realize that fulfilling your duty is the right choice, the honorable choice for the future of our kingdoms. Don't expect me to disappear."

"You won't change my mind."

"Maybe not," he says. "But I have to try."

I nod. We're both being steadfast in what we have to do. For half a second I wonder which of us is going to succeed in the end.

Then, with a nod, he stands.

"Tell Dosinia I said good night," he says, and he turns and heads for the door. "I'll see you tomorrow."

It seems wrong to let him just walk away. He was one of my closest friends for many years, and he is in a strange town for the first time.

"Do you have somewhere to stay?" I ask.

He stops in the doorway. "No."

My heart melts a little. He took a big risk coming here, with no plan except talking to me. And I just shot him down. I can't send him out, alone, into the Seaview night. Not when there are sheets to spare and a sofa bed in the living room.

"I'm sure Aunt Rachel will insist you stay with us." I don't know if I make the offer because he is my childhood friend or because, maybe, one tiny little part of me wants to give him every opportunity to succeed in convincing me to agree to his plan. Like Doe hoping I can help her get over her hate. It's hard to toss aside a lifetime of duty. "The couch converts into a very comfortable bed."

"I would be"—Tellin turns back to face me, a sober expression on his face—"very grateful."

"Come on," I say, trying to break the tension, "I'll show you where the linens are."

As Tellin follows me to the hall closet, I can't stop thinking about his what-if. And wondering whether the two of us, united, could turn it into reality.

"What do you mean, he's staying with you?" Quince asks through the phone.

I wiggle my tail fin to send small waves of salty suds up over my torso. "He doesn't have anywhere else to go," I explain. "He is one of my oldest friends. I can't just throw him out into the street."

Quince mumbles something that sounds like "*I* can."

I haven't told Quince about Tellin's proposal. I can just imagine the results. Quince would probably grab Tellin and throw him headfirst out the front door. At this point, it's better that he not know. It's not like it's going to become an issue.

"You're just mad because he ate all the cookies," I tease. "Aunt Rachel and I will make a double batch tomorrow."

Knock, knock, knock, knock, kno—

"What?" I shout at the door. Instead of an answer, I see the door handle turn. "Dosinia!"

Who else would just barge in on my bath? Certainly not Tellin or Aunt Rachel.

Sure enough, her blond head leans in.

"Your aunt said you could show me how to communicate without a message bubble or messenger gull."

I sigh back against the porcelain.

"Just a second, okay?"

Rather than the glib response I've come to expect from her, she quietly says, "Okay."

I hear the door click shut.

"Gotta go?" Quince asks.

"Yeah," I say. "Doe needs to use the phone."

Neither of us wants to hang up. After a few seconds of listening to each other's breathing, Quince says, "She'll come around."

"I hope so." Closing my eyes, I focus on my transformation, returning to my land legs. "I'm not sure what to do if she doesn't."

"She will," he insists.

"How can you know that?"

"Because I have faith in you," he says, and I can hear the grin in his voice, "And I have faith in love."

"Me too," I say, echoing his smile.

"I'll see you in the morning."

"Yes please."

We exchange I-love-yous and good-nights before hanging up. I pull the plug from the bath, splash the soap film off my chest, and climb out as the water swirls down the drain.

"Doe," I call out as I wrap a towel around my dripping body. "I'm read—"

"Great." The door pops open, and she steps into the bathroom. "I need to communicate with Brody."

With a sigh at her near-invasion of privacy, I hand her the receiver and explain how to dial the phone. She stares at the buttons, confused. Pushing it back at me, she says, "You do it."

I start to take the phone but stop myself. If Doe is going to learn how to appreciate humans, she's going to have to learn how to *be* human. "No," I insist. "You dial it or you don't talk to him."

She throws me an evil look but carefully pushes the talk button. As I recite Brody's number from memory—at least three years of crushing left me with something useful—she dials, only messing up and having to start over once. When she's finished, I indicate that she needs to hold the receiver to her ear.

"It's buzzing," she says, sounding concerned.

"Ringing," I correct. "That means you did it right."

Her attention shifts as the ringing stops. I can hear someone say something on the other end.

Doe asks, "May I speak with Brody, please?" There's a pause and then, "It's Dosinia."

Holding her hand over the mouthpiece, she says to me, "His mother is fetching him."

I smile.

Until she adds, "You can leave now."

My first thought is to strangle her. Her attention is back on the phone; she'd never see it coming. But that would leave Brody heartbroken by an unsevered bond. I couldn't do that to him.

Besides, I don't have the energy to do it right.

In the end, I just clench my teeth, take a deep breath, and leave the room. Doe slams the door behind me. Maybe, if I ask really nicely, Aunt Rachel will get me my own line. Or, even better, a cell phone. Though I can only imagine the cell phone company laughing when I bring in my soaking phone for replacement.

Maybe I should just stick with the land line.

Suppressing the temptation to listen in on her conversation—if she doesn't know how to dial a phone, she can't possibly understand about extensions—I head to my room and hold the door open for Prithi to join me. Traitor that she is, she's stationed outside the bathroom instead of following me.

"I'm the one who feeds you, you know."

She gives me a wistful look, like she wishes she could be in two places at once, and then turns and presses her nose to the crack under the bathroom door.

"Fine." I swing the door shut behind me.

After retrieving my rainbow pajamas from beneath my pillow and trading them for my towel wrap, I sit down at my desk and pull out markers and a blank sheet of paper. Using an exercise we learned in freshman English, I fold the paper in half lengthwise and prepare to make a pros-and-cons list. I use a purple marker to draw a line down the middle. Then I title each column and begin filling them in.

Accept Tellin's Proposal	Reject Tellin's Proposal
Duty	Love
Daddy	Aunt Rachel
My kingdom	Myself
Legacy	Future
Living up to my potential	Discover new potential
Responsibility	Dedication
The people of Thalassinia	Quince
Leading my people underwater	Protecting my people from above

I'm not sure what I'd hoped to accomplish by making this list. Maybe I thought one side of the decision would far outweigh the other and I wouldn't have to fret about it anymore.

The truth is there are valid reasons for me to make either choice. The only difference is . . . it's a choice I've already made. I'm giving up my title and living on land, living with my human half and forging a future with the boy I love.

Without another thought, I crumple the list and toss it into the trash. That's the end of that mental debate.

Then why do I still feel so adrift?

$\mathcal{B}$y lunch the next day, Doe and Brody are back in each other's laps. By Wednesday afternoon I'm ready to throw them both back into the ocean. If only the waters of south Florida were chilly enough to cool them off.

When I stomp through the kitchen door after school and find them sharing one of the dining chairs, I stomp right on through to the living room before flinging my backpack to the ground.

I know this is what I wanted to happen, but does it all have to be so in-my-face?

"Something wrong?" Tellin asks.

I glance—okay, *glare*—at the armchair where he's been spending practically all his time since he got here on Monday. He's mentioned his proposal a couple of times, but he hasn't been pushing the issue.

"No," I snap. "I mean, yes. Not really. I just—" I shake my head. "I don't need to see my baby cousin making all lovey-dovey with my ex-crush."

I flop on the couch, jerk open the zipper on my bag, and pull out my SAT prep guide. Flipping it open to the next sample test, I slam it on the coffee table and slide down onto the floor to begin.

"You've been spending a lot of your time with that book," Tellin observes. "May I ask why?"

"Because," I explain, trying to scan the rules for the first section, even though I should have them memorized by now, "the test is on Saturday and if I don't do really, really well, then I won't get into college because my grades have been pretty pitiful because until three weeks ago I thought I didn't need to worry about a future on land because I was going to become a mer queen and spend my years ruling over Thalassinia instead of studying literature and American Government."

A long silence fills the room after my mini rant. Finally Tellin laughs and says, "Now tell me your true feelings."

I slump. "I know it's not the most important thing in the world," I admit. Things like war and famine and ocean warming come to mind. "But if I want to protect the oceans in an official, scientific capacity, then I need higher education. I can't become a marine biologist without at least a college degree."

"You can help the oceans in another way," he says quietly.

I guess I should be thankful he's been quiet as long as he has. Maybe he's been patiently waiting for the right moment.

Now is *not* that moment.

"Tell me why." I lay my pencil down in the open seam of the study guide. "Why do you think this is such a great idea?"

"I told you why."

"You told me *a* reason," I argue. "But I don't think you've told me *your* reason."

"Lily," Tellin says, sinking down onto the floor next to me, "you are the best hope for Thalassinia's future. For the future freedom of all the mer kingdoms. With our forces united, we will be able to enact positive change—"

"This is everything you said before." And everything that tugged at the lifetime of duty that Daddy trained into me. But something is missing. "You have another reason. I can sense it."

"You're wrong," he says with another laugh. "I have been raised to honor duty before all else, just like you. I can imagine no better way to fulfill our duties than by joining our kingdoms for the greater good."

"I just don't think I can—"

"You know that's why my father stopped speaking to yours, right?"

"What?" I jerk back. "No. Why?"

"King Whelk wanted to enter us into an arranged marriage," Tellin explains. "My father disagreed. He wanted me to seek out my true love, my true mermate. When your father insisted, mine severed relations."

"That's impossible." I shake my head, not able to wrap my mind around the idea of Daddy wanting to sign my future away on a piece of paper. It seems so unlike him.

"It's not," Tellin says. "This is another reason why I think my plan is a good one. It is what your father has wanted all along." His gaze drifts toward the front door, but I can tell he's not seeing anything. "As difficult as it is for me to admit, my father was wrong in this. Our union can only be for the best of both our kingdoms."

He makes it seem so tempting. The fact that I'm even considering the possibility is ridiculous. But, like we've always said . . . "What if?"

"What if," Tellin says, jumping on my opening, "we bonded and—"

"What if who bonded?"

"Quince!" I jump at the sound of his voice. He walks into the living room with a dark look on his face. And no wonder, if he heard what Tellin and I were talking about.

"I thought you were at work?" I ask, hopefully not sounding—or looking—guilty.

"I was," he says flatly. "There's a tropical storm coming in, so they closed the lumberyard." He throws Tellin a dark look. "What if who bonded?"

"It's just a game we used to play as guppies," I explain before Tellin can respond. He could only make the situation worse. "One of us starts a what-if, and then we keep going down that path, alternating what-ifs until we get to a conclusion. Or we start laughing too hard to continue."

"A game," Quince echoes. "So, in what what-if are the two of you bonded?"

"It's just a—"

Tellin interrupts. "I commented on how funny it would be if we had bonded as children," he lies. "We almost shared a first kiss once or twice, but Lily was always the levelheaded one." He grins at me. "Spurned my every advance."

I throw Tellin a grateful smile. Not that he and I were doing anything wrong, but still. My relationship with Quince—our official boyfriend-girlfriend relationship, anyway—is still pretty new. I don't want him worrying over something that would never happen.

Like Tellin said, I'm too levelheaded to do anything so impulsive.

Tellin, probably sensing the almost tangible tension in the room, stands, clears his throat, and excuses himself to the kitchen. Seconds later, he's fleeing the smoochfest he found there for the upstairs.

Quince, who has been standing, rigid and acting as the epicenter for all that anxiety, asks, "What was that really about?"

"Nothing. I told you, we just—"

"Save it," he says, cutting me off. "I know you better than anyone. I can tell when you're lying to me."

"It's not a lie." Not really. We *were* playing a game and, even though for half a second I might have maybe sorta thought about actually considering the idea, I wasn't really serious. I insist, "We were playing a game."

He looks at me for a minute, studying, trying to see through my words to decide if I'm telling the truth. Finally he closes his eyes and shakes his head. "Yeah, sorry. It's been a long day."

I cross the room and wrap my arms around his waist. "It's been a long month."

He gives me a quick hug and then leans back, nodding at the open study guide on the table. "You want some help?"

"Of course," I say, grasping at the safe topic of my SAT prep. As he settles, cross-legged, on the floor across the table, I ask, "Are you going to distract me by playing footsie?"

"Absolutely, princess," he says with a wink.

"Then I won't remember a thing."

"It's a samurai training technique," he teases, spinning the test prep book toward him. "I distract you as much as possible right now." He slides the book into his lap. "And you'll learn how to test through anything."

"Samurai, huh?" I tease back, relieved to return to our relaxed positions. "We won't get anything done."

He winks again and then gets down to business, reading the first question aloud. My good humor evaporates as I focus on trying to figure out the parallel relationship between dog and quadruped.

12

"*I*'m going to fail."

"You're not going to fail," Shannen replies patiently. "You can't *fail* the SATs." She signals a left turn, checks both ways, and then pulls out onto the street in front of school. Her wipers swish back and forth against the tropical downpour. "The worst you can get on each section is a two hundred, I think, but they don't assign letter grades."

"Fine," I whine. "I'm going to get two hundreds."

"You won't." She spares me a glance. "You'll do really well in the reading and writing sections."

With a groan, I drop my head into my hands, knocking it against the dashboard on the way. I just groan again and sink deeper into my freakout. I haven't had enough time to prepare. I've wasted too much of what time I did have. And I'm going to have a complete mental meltdown tomorrow when the test begins.

I'll be lucky if I can speak in complete sentences at my interview after.

"The test is in the morning," I complain. "I only have sixteen more hours to cram in some studying."

Shannen pulls to a complete stop before proceeding onto my street. "No more cramming," she says. "There have been countless studies that show the more you try to learn in the last few hours before an exam, the less you retain."

"Really?"

"In fact," she says, a slightly smug smile on her face, "they suggest that it will even make you forget things you already know."

"Oh, no," I cry. "Then no more studying."

"No more studying," Shannen agrees.

Well, at least that gives me a little more freedom for my Friday night. I was already bummed because Quince had to run errands for his mom and couldn't give me a ride home—not that I mind riding with Shannen, it's just become a routine for Quince and me. The thought of spending the whole night with my nose buried in a study guide was just sad.

At least now maybe Shannen and I can enjoy an evening of board games and well-buttered popcorn.

"Wait a second," I say as she speeds past my house. "You missed my turn."

"I thought we could swing by the grocery store and get some caramels." She steers onto Seaview's main shopping street. "Ever have caramel corn?"

"No," I say, intrigued. "Is it good?"

"It's amazing," she says, pulling into the store parking lot. Which happens to be right next to Mushu Sushi, my favorite land-based sushi restaurant. I give their red-lacquered doors a yearning glance.

"Want to grab dinner first?" Shannen asks.

Sushi is not her favorite, so I know she must have seen my longing look.

"Nah," I say, trying to be a good friend. "It's okay." The OPEN sign next to their front door is dark. "Besides, looks like they're closed."

"Let's check to make sure. I wouldn't say no to some edamame," Shannen says, jumping out of the car and dashing toward the restaurant to escape the rain.

"Okay." I shrug and follow her, never one to turn down a plateful of sushi goodness. I move slowly, letting the water cover me with its soothing energy. By the time I reach the awning, I look a little bedraggled but I feel wonderful.

Despite the dark sign, Mushu's front door swings open easily when Shannen pushes. She throws me a mischievous smile before walking in, holding the door open behind her.

Curious, I follow her inside.

"Surprise!!!"

Shouts bombard me from all directions.

I slam my palm against my chest before my heart can beat its way out. "Holy bananafish, you guys!"

192

"Happy birthday," Shannen says, handing me a box wrapped with yellow paper and curl upon curl of orange ribbon.

I take the box, still in shock and still staring around the room at everyone gathered in the tiny entryway. Besides Shannen, Aunt Rachel is there, beaming, and Quince, of course. He's got that boy-did-we-get-you look on his face, and that makes me smile more than anything. Next to him, Brody and Doe are joined at the hip, and a little ways to the side, Tellin is lounging against the wall, which is paneled with narrow strips of a very red wood.

"We knew you couldn't be here on your actual birthday," Aunt Rachel explains, "so we thought we'd surprise you with an early party."

The hostess arrives at her podium, grabs a stack of menus, and leads us to the private dining room in the back. Someone has transformed it into an underwater dream.

"This is just . . ." I take in all the decorations—streamers curling down from the ribbon in half a dozen shades of blue and green; big party-store cutouts of starfish, sea horses, and tropical fish; and tiny twinkling blue and green lights circling the room. My eyes tear, and I feel the emotion tighten around my throat. I take a quick breath to regain my control before saying, "Magical. Thank you." Realizing that this could not have been the effort of just one or two of my friends and family, I add, "Everyone."

"What are we waiting for?" Quince asks, rubbing his

palms together. "Let's eat."

He holds out the chair at the head of the table, motioning for me to sit there. When I do, he takes the seat to my right. Everyone fills in around the table, and the waiter starts bringing in sushi.

A tray of cone-shaped shrimp tempura and California temaki.

A beautiful platter of New York and Philadelphia maki.

A rainbow array of anago, himachi, and toro nigiri.

This is what birthday bliss is all about.

When the waiter pops his head in to see if we want more, everyone groans. I exchange a look along the length of the table with Tellin—the only person at the table who could possibly keep up with me when it comes to sushi consumption—and we share an omigod-I'm-so-full look.

"I couldn't eat another morsel," I announce.

Sounds of agreement come from everyone at the table. The waiter nods and disappears.

"Now," Aunt Rachel says, reaching beneath her seat and pulling out a very small box wrapped in homemade purple paper, "it's time for presents."

Everyone cheers and I blush. This is my least favorite part about human birthdays. I get so embarrassed. Under the sea a birthday is just a celebration, not a gift-giving occasion. Getting gifts is great, but I get squirmy under the spotlight, everyone watching while you carefully—or carelessly— open your package.

But as a full-time land resident, I'll just have to get over it.

Aunt Rachel sets her gift in front of her and says, "I'd like to save mine for last, if that's okay."

"Open mine first," Shannen says, nodding at the yellow-and-orange package next to my water glass.

"Okay." I smile as I reach for the box.

"There's a tradition," Aunt Rachel explains to Doe and Tellin, since they probably don't know, "that if the birthday girl tears the wrapping paper on her first present, she gets as many spankings as she is old."

Being fully aware of this tradition—and Aunt Rachel's determination to uphold it—I use my fingernail to slit the tape securing the yellow wrapping paper. In seconds, I've dewrapped the gift and handed the paper to Aunt Rachel for inspection.

"Sadly," Aunt Rachel says with a mock frown, "Lily has managed to avoid getting spanked for four birthdays running."

Everyone laughs. I take the opportunity of their distraction to open the white box that contains Shannen's gift. Inside, on a bed of yellow tissue paper, is a bright orange calculator with yellow keys. I lift it out and play with a few of the buttons.

"It's for the SATs tomorrow," Shannen explains.

"It's perfect," I say, pushing out of my chair and giving her a hug. "Every time I have to solve a math problem, I'll think of you. It will help me focus more."

195

Shannen beams.

"Mine next," Doe says, passing an unwrapped box down the table.

Sinking back into my chair, I take the box. This is momentous. She's participating in a human ritual. It must be a sign of progress, right?

I give Doe a small smile before pulling off the lid.

I gasp.

"I just thought," she says, "that since you made one for Quincy, maybe you'd like one, too."

"Doe," I say, full of emotion as I pull out the inch-wide sapphire blue sand dollar. "It's beautiful."

I hold up the necklace for everyone to see. Quince reaches beneath his black T-shirt and pulls out the matching necklace I made for him just a few weeks ago. The smile he gives me might seem perfectly ordinary, but it's not. It says, There's hope for Doe yet.

I completely agree.

"Thank you, Dosinia," I say sincerely. "I cannot imagine a more perfect gift."

She rolls her eyes and shrugs, as if my compliment means nothing. I can tell she's proud of herself. Besides, with her powers revoked, she can't flash-freeze sand dollars anymore. She either planned this ahead of time or asked for help.

The girl may pretend like she doesn't care about anyone but herself, but she's proving that's not true. In more ways than one.

Brody hands down an envelope. "Now mine."

I rip open the top of the plain brown envelope, curious as to what kind of present might be in here. When I pull out a sheet of paper and read the contents, I realize what his gift is.

"No way," I say, rereading the letter. "Are you serious?"

"As Olympic gold."

"What?" Shannen asks.

Aunt Rachel asks, "What is it?"

I clear my throat and read the letter. "Dear Teachers. The following students will be absent from class on Thursday and Friday to attend the boys' state swimming championships: Brody Bennett, Kevin Velasquez, Raymond Flynn, and team manager Lily Sanderson. Please gather their homework assignments so they may complete them on time. If you have any questions, please call my office. Coach Hill."

"I don't get it," Shannen says.

Doe asks, "What's the gift?"

So excited I might just burst, my gaze meets Brody's across the table. "I get to go to State."

The silence around the table seems to say, "And . . . ?"

"Managers never get to go to State," I explain, "since it's usually just the coach and a couple of swimmers. This is"—I shake my head at Brody—"awesome. Thank you."

In my three years as swim team manager, it's always been a bittersweet end to the season—having to hang up my record book while a handful of swimmers got to travel to Orlando for the state meet. It's awesome that, as a senior, I'll get to go, too.

Brody just earned triple points. Not only for getting me the letter, but also for knowing how much it would mean to me. Maybe he wasn't quite as self-absorbed as I thought.

Maybe this gift-getting thing is worth the torture after all.

I look around expectantly, wondering whose gift will wow me next.

Without saying a word, Quince pulls a small box from the inside pocket of his jacket. He slides it across the red tablecloth.

My eyes meet his as I pick up the box and pull off the red ribbon. It feels like we haven't had much time together as boyfriend-girlfriend since I came back, but the look in his eyes is all I need to see the promise of a long future between us.

I absently lift off the lid and reach inside. My fingers curl around a cold metal object.

Glancing down, I find a starfish-shaped silver key ring.

"It's beautiful," I whisper.

He leans close. "Turn it over."

On the back, inscribed in a delicately curving script, are the words *Forever, princess. I love you.*

Tears instantly fill my eyes.

"I love you, too," I mouth.

"What?" Shannen demands, reaching across the table

to take the starfish. When she reads the inscription, she's struck speechless.

The key ring makes the rounds of the table, eliciting shrugs from the boys and sighs from the girls. When it makes its way back to my palm, I clutch it close to my heart.

"Thank you," I say, though words can't entirely express what I'm feeling.

"After that," Aunt Rachel announces, "it seems apropos to give you my gift next."

She lifts the flecked purple package off the table and hands it to me.

Her eyes are wide with pride and expectation as I peel off the wrapping. It's quite a small box with hardly any weight to it. Maybe it's a gift card? I could use a trip to the mall for some summer beach staples. Flip-flops, bikinis, tank tops. I'm always up for a shopping spree.

But when I pull the lid off the box, it is not a gift card resting on the tie-dye pink-and-purple tissue. It's a key.

I don't get it. I already have a key to the house, both front and back doors. There aren't any other locks in my life, except for the combination on my locker at school. No key required.

And it's not exactly shaped like a house key.

"What's it for?" I ask.

Quince smiles, taking the key and inspecting it like he's never seen it before, but I get the feeling he has. "A Toyota Corolla, if I had to guess."

Aunt Rachel nods.

"A car?" I gasp.

"Your father and I agreed," she says, "that you will need your own transportation once you begin college."

If I begin college, I almost say. The pressure of tomorrow's SATs is enough to make me think I'll never get accepted.

But today is a celebration, and I refuse to dwell on the negative. And besides . . . I have a car!

"A car! It's an amazing gift, Aunt Rachel," I say. I wrap her in a tight hug. "I just hope I can learn how to drive."

"I'll teach you," Quince says.

I raise my brows. "Just like you're teaching me to ride Princess?"

When I came back to Seaview, he promised to teach me to ride his motorcycle. Let's just say that the couple lessons we've had have ended roughly. No blood, but a few scratches—on both me and Princess. One more trip into the garbage cans, and Quince will rescind his promise to teach me.

"By the time I'm done with you," he says, "you'll drive like a NASCAR champ."

I grin back at him. If anyone can teach me how to handle a car, it's Quince.

I don't see how this surprise party could get any better.

At the other end of the table, Tellin shoves back in his chair and stands.

"I regret to say I have no gift for the birthday girl," he

says. Reaching for his water glass, he continues, "So I would like to offer a toast instead."

Everyone else stands and lifts their glasses as Tellin speaks. I stand, too, because I'm not sure what else to do.

"To my guppyhood friend," he says. "The princess of our hearts. A kind and generous and openhearted person who would give up anything and everything to be with the one she loves." He flicks me an unreadable look. "Even her title. To Lily."

He lifts his glass, and everyone else says, "To Lily," and follows suit.

Everyone except me. And Quince.

They've missed the subtle shark attack Tellin lobbed into the room.

"What does he mean?" Quince demands.

I swallow hard. "About what?"

I throw Tellin a glare—does he know what he's done?—but he just smiles and lowers himself back into his chair. He knows exactly what is about to happen. This is all part of his plan, part of his proposal.

"You know what," Quince says, his voice deceptively calm. "Giving up your title? He's not serious."

"Quince," I say, glancing around at the eager eyes watching the shipwreck in progress, "can we talk about this late—"

"What does he mean, Lily?" His voice has taken on that tone that says, Tell me the truth right now or I'm walking.

"By Thalassinian law," I begin, "any royal princess who is

not bonded by her eighteenth birthday . . ." It's hard to say this out loud, but I have to. "Loses her title and her place in the succession."

Quince's Caribbean blue eyes bore into me, his brows drawn together in a look of utter confusion. He shakes his head, like this can't possibly make sense.

"As of midnight on Tuesday," I explain, "I will no longer be Thalassinia's future queen."

Everyone still standing drops into their chairs, except Quince and me, accompanied by various sighs and gasps. Doe already knew this, of course, but it's a shocker to the rest of the party.

The look in Quince's eyes could melt a hole in the hull of a battleship.

He's about to say something when the waiter pops in and asks, "Are we ready for cake?"

I don't take my eyes off Quince, who closes his eyes, shakes his head, and drops back into his chair. Whatever argument we're about to have isn't over, but I get the feeling he doesn't want to ruin the party. At least not for everyone else.

"Yes," Aunt Rachel says with forced cheerfulness. "Now would be an excellent time for cake."

I slowly lower into my chair, not bothering to pretend I don't know why Quince is upset. This is the one teeny-tiny part of the staying-on-land bargain that I've neglected to mention. I was going to wait until after my birthday, until after Tuesday and the ritual was done, before telling him all about it. Partly because this is the reaction I expected. Partly because the decision is a personal one. Mine and mine alone.

Thanks a lot, Tellin. I throw a glare his way just as the lights in the room go dark and the waiter, followed by the hostess and two sushi chefs, walks in with a candlelit birthday cake.

As everyone breaks into a chorus of "Happy Birthday," I try to enjoy the moment. To enjoy celebrating my eighteenth year with my closest land friends and family. But even though he's forcing out the words, all I feel is anger rolling off Quince, in tsunami-sized waves.

"Make a wish," Aunt Rachel says.

I take one look at the round white cake, decorated with blue-and-green waves and the words HAPPY BIRTHDAY, LILY, and tears fill my eyes. Closing them quickly before anyone notices, I suck in a breath, quickly compose my wish, and blow.

When I open my eyes, the candles are smoking and everyone is clapping. Everyone but Quince.

There's still hope for my wish, though. Because I didn't wish for something as fleeting as for Quince to not be mad at me. I wasn't about to waste the potential birthday magic on something that can be solved with a very long conversation.

No, I've been thinking about my wish a lot in the last

couple weeks, preparing for this moment. In the end, it wasn't hard to figure out what I really wanted.

My wish is for Quince to be able to return to Thalassinia with me one day.

Let's hope birthday-cake magic has some bite.

Aunt Rachel drives me home in my car—*my car!*—because I'm in no state for a driving lesson. Between the pending fight with Quince, tomorrow's SATs, my interview, and the truth of the situation behind Tellin's news flash (aka *un-becoming a princess*), I'm a mess of nerves and nausea.

"It's a standard transmission," Aunt Rachel explains, moving the big stick in the middle of the car as we pull into our driveway, "which might take some extra getting used to, but it's better in the long run."

I nod absently, but my mind is on Quince. He's leaning against the front porch of his house, waiting for me, looking full-on rebel boy in his beaten-up jeans, snug-but-not-too-tight black T-shirt, and lovingly scuffed biker boots. He is so breathtakingly handsome that I don't want to get out of the car and ruin the image.

Even in the faint glow of streetlamps, through the drizzling rain, from a moving car, I can read the tension in his shoulders.

I am such an idiot. Why didn't I tell him the truth before? I never lied exactly, I just neglected to tell him something. Something kinda big, true, but it's my decision. I knew what I was signing up for.

Still, we're supposed to be partners in this relationship. We're supposed to share everything, and I didn't hold up my end of the bargain. I'm about to pay the price for that.

Aunt Rachel puts the car in park and shuts it off.

"I'll be inside in a little while," I say. As I reluctantly push open the passenger door, I whisper, "I hope."

"Be understanding," she advises. "This was a big piece of news, and he probably feels a little blindsided."

"I know." Boy, do I know.

She pats me on the thigh in encouragement, and then I climb out of the car, into the drizzle. I straighten my shoulders, deciding to let him have the first words in this discussion. It won't help for me to begin all defensive and full of excuses.

I round the corner of his house to find he hasn't moved. He is staring, unseeing, at the mailbox at the end of his front walk, oblivious to the rain. I don't say a word, just take the spot next to him on the porch rail and lean back. Waiting.

I don't have to wait long.

"Were you ever going to tell me?"

His voice is far more calm than I'd expected.

Deciding that honesty is the best possible path at this point, I admit, "I don't know."

He forces a laugh. "You don't know?"

"If it came up," I explain, "I would have told you. After

my birthday, probably. But, truthfully, I didn't think it was any of your concern."

"None of my concern?" he roars. "You're planning on giving up your royal future for me, and you think it's none of my concern?"

"My decision," I argue, "was not entirely about you. It's also about my mom, about the human heritage that I'm only just beginning to understand."

I sense his mood softening at the mention of my mom. Even though his dad's a deadbeat, he still has both parents around, so he's extra sympathetic about my losing her before I even knew her.

"And also about Aunt Rachel and Shannen," I continue. "And about me. About having choices in my life, my future, and wanting more than a lifetime of negotiations and decrees and royal events and—"

"Bull." He crosses his arms over his chest, and I have to stop myself from wrapping my hands around one well-developed biceps. "You're giving up too much," he says. "Just because you think all that stuff sounds boring right now doesn't mean it always will. You're too young to make that kind of permanent decision."

I take a deep breath. "You were ready to make that decision for yourself."

When we were bonded and my feelings for him were just beginning, he begged me to preserve the bond, because he had already loved me for so long. Even when I told him what he would be giving up—his future on land, being there for his mom, everything he had always known—he still wanted to go through with it.

He was willing to sacrifice everything for me. But he doesn't want me to do the same for him.

"That's different," he argues.

"How?" I demand, pushing away from the porch and moving into his line of sight. The rain is soaking my hair, and I shove it behind my ears to keep it from sticking to my face. "You were ready to give up everything for the complete unknown of the ocean and an uncertain future with me. I've already been living on land for almost four years, so I know what I'm getting into up here." I step close and rest my palms on his forearms. "And I know what I'm getting into with you."

For a moment I think he's going to relent, admit to being foolish, and take me in his arms for some makeup making out. But I sense the instant his mood shifts. Back to anger.

"You're being a fool," he barks. "I won't let you give up your world, your royal future, for *me*."

He uncrosses his arms, dislodging my hands and breaking our point of contact. Without another word, he grabs his leather jacket off the railing, shoves away from the porch, and heads around to the driveway between our houses.

I follow, my flip-flops slipping on the wet grass, seriously worried for the first time. He's pushing me away as hard as he can.

"Why?" I shout, following him up the gravel path. "What's the difference if you make the sacrifice or I do? The end result is the same."

He doesn't answer as he shrugs into his jacket. He grabs the helmet hanging from his motorcycle handlebars and slips it in place over his head.

"It's different," he finally says as he buckles the strap into place, "because you're worth it."

"And you're not?"

"I'm not."

He turns the key, and Princess roars to life. Even as the sound assaults my ears, I can't move. My eyes fill with tears, and blinking only seems to make it worse. At least he can't see them in the rain.

How can he say that? How can he *think* that? Does he really think so little of himself that he can't imagine anyone making a sacrifice for him? My heart starts breaking into tiny little pieces, breaking for him.

Suddenly I don't care anymore about the fight or my renunciation or Tellin's proposal or anything except wanting him to realize how exceptional he is.

"You're wrong," I shout over Princess's muffler. "You're more than worth—"

"Why is Tellin here?"

"What?" I ask, startled by the change of subject.

"He's not just here for a visit, Lily." Quince refuses to look at me. "Why is he really here?"

I take a deep breath and wipe the water off my face. There's no way I'm going to lie to him. Not now, not ever again. My lie of omission is already costing me too much.

"He wants to bond with me," I yell. "In name only, a bond of convenience. So I can become crown princess and eventually queen. So he and I can rule together."

Quince sits silent, staring down at the gray and white gravel, the thunderous roar of his motorcycle echoing between our houses. I don't think I'm breathing. Finally, after what feels like a lifetime, he turns to face me.

"Bond with Tellin," he says, soft but hard, and somehow I hear every word despite the noise. "Stay a princess. Become a queen." He starts backing down the driveway, and I have to step back to protect my bare toes. "Forget about me."

I can only manage to shake my head as he increases his speed, zipping down the driveway, into the street, and then, shifting into gear, speeding out into the night. I race down the gravel path, reaching the sidewalk just as Quince disappears around the corner at the next intersection.

I'm not sure how long I stand there, letting the rain soak me to the core, staring at the spot where he disappeared from view. Eventually the drizzle fades into a mist and then stops entirely. My skin prickles with eelflesh in the evening chill. The tears streaming down my cheeks dry into sad streaks. I'm not sure I blink at all until I feel a pair of soft hands on my shoulders.

"It's time to come in, dear," Aunt Rachel says. "You need

your rest for tomorrow."

I feel myself nod, but everything else is numb. Sometime later I realize I'm in bed, wide-awake and staring at the ceiling. I'm not sure what upsets me more: the fact that Quince left me, or the fact that he thinks so poorly of himself that he felt the need to.

One thing is certain. I can't possibly follow his instructions. Nothing on earth will ever make me forget about him.

13

"*F*or this section of the test you may use a calculator," the SAT administrator explains, reading from the script she has to recite before each part of the test.

I reach down into my bag and pull out Shannen's birthday present. As the administrator drones on, thoughts of Quince and Tellin and Doe and Brody and my future and my past keep trying to push their way into my brain, but I shove them away. I have to. When the test is over, I can soak in my worries. Until then, I need to maintain my focus. Whatever the future brings, I want to have choices. Can't have choices on land without college.

"You may open your test booklet to the math section. You have twenty-five minutes to complete this section. You may begin."

Forcing all thoughts beyond the world contained in the packet of papers before me to disappear, I tell myself I exist only for math. Groan. But every time I start to read a question, it's like the words begin to swim around. It takes me a few questions to realize it's because my eyes are swimming with tears. How am I ever going to do decently on the test if I can't even read the questions?

When the administrator instructs us to put our pencils down almost half an hour later, I've managed to finish almost all of the questions. I have serious doubts that I even read them correctly, let alone answered them with any degree of success. And to be honest, I don't really care. In the scale of things, my fight with Quince—one that might not be easily resolved—seems far more important than a single test. There will be other tests. There can never be another Quince.

After two breaks and another three equally incomplete test sections, the administrator finally announces that the test is over.

Cheers go up around the room, but all I can do is slump my shoulders—in relief and in anticipation of what I have to face beyond the cafeteria doors.

Shannen is waiting for me in the parking lot when I step out into the bright sun. Yesterday's rain is gone without a trace. Since I haven't magically learned how to drive overnight, she brought me to school early this morning and promised to pick me up after.

"So . . . ," she says. "How'd it go?"

"Froggin' crabtastic," I answer with a shrug.

"I'm sure you did fine." She slides into the driver's seat and starts the car. "Should we go celebrate?"

As if I'm in the mood to celebrate anything. I'm not even in the mood to talk. I just want to go home and see if Quince is there so we can work through this. I have to believe that we can. The alternative is unacceptable.

But I have an unavoidable responsibility to take care of first.

I shake my head as I drop into the passenger seat. "Can't."

"Plans?"

I heave a sigh at the thought of what I have to do. It's not the most important thing to me at the moment, but it's time sensitive.

"Tonight is the new moon," I explain. "If I don't separate Doe and Brody before moonrise, their bond will become permanent."

A permanently bonded Doe and Brody couldn't be good for anyone.

"How do you do that?" Shannen asks. "Separate them, I mean."

"Daddy gave me the power to perform the ritual." I tug at the seat belt where it rubs against my neck. "All I have to do is say the magic words and get the happy couple to sign the separation papers."

"No big, then."

"Nope," I agree. "No big."

As we drive the few blocks from school to my house in

silence, I keep thinking about the next thing on my list of worries. Making up with Quince. This isn't our first fight—heck, we've been fighting since long before we started going out—but this one feels more real. More significant. I don't want it to linger any longer than necessary.

"How about lunch tomorrow?" Shannen asks, pulling her car to a stop at the end of my sidewalk. "Before you head home for your birthday celebration."

"Sure," I say, unbuckling and opening the door. "Sounds great."

"I'll come by around one to pick you up."

"Perfect."

I wave good-bye as Shannen pulls away from the curb.

When I push open the kitchen door, the house is eerily quiet. With four people living in our house right now, there's usually at least some sign of another occupant.

"Aunt Rachel?" I call out. "Doe? Tellin?" When I get no response, I wonder if every living creature in the house has disappeared. "Prithi?"

At that I get a reassuring *meow*.

There are no signs of life in the kitchen, so I head into the living room. It looks more deserted than usual. Not that Tellin brought any belongings with him, but it feels like he's moved out. My suspicion is confirmed when I read the note he left on the coffee table.

See you at your birthday ball.

Well, that's one worry off my shoulders for the moment.

Next I head upstairs to hunt for Doe. She must know that we have to perform the separation tonight, so why would she disappear like this? Clearly she has, though. She's not anywhere in the house, as evidenced by the fact that Prithi is trailing my every step.

It's late afternoon already. In a few hours it will be too late.

I grab the upstairs phone—the one I'm usually dropping in the bathwater—and dial Brody's home number.

"This is Lily Sanderson," I say when his mom answers the phone. "Is Brody home?"

"No, dear," she says. "I think he went out with your cousin."

"Did he say where?"

"Not specifically," she says, "but he took towels and his swim trunks. Maybe the pool?"

Unlikely. Doe shares my merfolk allergy to chlorine. My guess is they've headed to the beach. Why, I don't know, because it's not like Doe can follow him under the ocean. But it's salt water. And they both see it as home.

"Okay, I'll try there," I tell Mrs. Bennett. "Thanks."

Great. Now I have to find a way to the beach. I guess that makes this as good a time as ever to talk with Quince—to make up and to get transportation. I grab the separation papers from my room and shove them into my back pocket before heading out. As I crunch across the gravel driveway separating our houses, I mentally compose what I'll say to

215

him. *"I'm sorry. I should have told you. But it's my decision and I love you. I could never leave."*

By the time I stomp up his front steps I think I've got my speech set. I knock on the big white door and wait. As the door swings open, I paste an apologetic smile on my face and start to say, "I'm s—"

"Hello, Lily," Quince's mom says.

"Mrs. Fletcher?" I guess I'm just surprised to find her answering the door. It seems like she's always at work or sleeping—she pulls the night shift at the factory, so she sleeps during the day.

"Janet," she says, offering me a haggard smile. "Please, call me Janet."

I nod, but can't bring myself to call her by her first name. "Is Quince home?"

Her thin, aged-beyond-her-years face transforms into a frown. "He didn't tell you?"

A bad feeling thumps into my stomach like a punch in the gut. "Tell me what?"

"He left." She braces an arm against the doorjamb, as if she needs the support. "Took off up the coast last night." She shakes her head sadly. "Probably to visit his father."

"Oh." That's all I can manage to say around the tear-clogged lump in my throat.

"I thought he would have told you."

My eyes are watering faster than I can blink the tears away. "We're kind of having a fight," I explain. "I didn't tell

216

him something and he . . . he's pretty angry."

"You weren't—" She pauses, like she has to figure out the best way to say something. "Unfaithful?"

"No!" I hurry to explain. "Nothing like that. Never."

"Then you shouldn't worry." Her haggard face softens as she smiles. "My son may have a hot temper from time to time, but if you haven't violated his code of loyalty, then everything will be fine once he cools off."

"I hope so." I'm not so sure, but I definitely hope so.

"He loves you," she says plainly. "For him, that's everything."

I don't have any choice but to believe her. That's how I feel, too, so I have to believe that's how Quince feels. Besides, it's not like I can go after him. I have to find a way to get to Doe and Brody first.

Quince and I can sort things out later. I hope.

If only I could convince myself that my lie of omission *wasn't* a violation of his code of loyalty, as his mom put it. Maybe it was more of a betrayal than he can forgive.

"Mrs. Fletcher—" At her frown, I amend, "Janet. Do you think you could give me a ride somewhere?"

"Sure, honey." She reaches back inside and grabs her purse off the floor. "Where do you need to go?"

"Thanks Mrs. Fle—uh, Janet." I wave as Quince's mom pulls out of the Seaview Beach parking lot.

Turning to face the beach, I search out my catch. Brody's

Camaro is parked in the corner of the lot, so I know they're here. I scan the sand. There is a family with small children picnicking down the beach to the south and a pair of joggers heading north along the surf line. No sign of Doe or Brody.

On a hunch, I head toward the pier.

As my feet squish through the sand, I think about what Quince's mom said. That love is everything to him. That he'll forgive my lie of omission.

But what if she's wrong? What if he thinks I'm untrustworthy and he can never believe in me again? What if, even if we get back together, he always wonders if there's something I'm not telling him? What if he is racked with doubts and suspicions every time I head home for a weekend? He can't go with me, so he'll never be able to see for himself.

By the time I've reached the spot where the ocean meets the pier, I'm practically in tears again. I just wish Quince was here so we could talk this out. Whenever I think through things in my head, they always go a little out of control.

"Lily?"

I snap out of my mental whirlpool at the sound of Doe's voice.

"What are you doing here?" she asks.

Sinking shoulder deep in the water, still fully clothed, I finally see her and Brody tucked behind a pylon halfway down the pier.

"What am I doing here?" I echo, shaking myself back into the moment. "I'm here to perform the separation. In case you forgot, the bond will become permanent with tonight's new moon."

"I—" Her piercing blue gaze flicks to Brody and then back to me. "I didn't forget."

"Then why did you disappear?" I ask, rolling my eyes.

Sometimes, I swear, it's like she's turned off her capacity for rational thought. First the trident incident, then bonding with Brody in the first place, and now this. I wish she would grow up already and stop leaving her problems on my doorstep.

I swim over to their spot and pull the separation papers out of my back pocket. Thankfully they're on kelpaper or they'd be ruined by the salt water now soaking my capris. "Let's get this over with."

Neither of them says a word.

With my toes just reaching the sand below, I find the page with the words of the ritual written in Daddy's scrawling script.

My eyes scan over the page until I find the spot where I'm supposed to begin. I only have to blink away my tears twice to read the words on the pages.

"A mistake was made," I begin. "Now let the bond fade. These two once united shall soon be div—"

"Don't."

Doe's soft whisper stops me cold. I don't think a shout would have startled me nearly as much as that quiet plea. It might be the first truly serious thing Doe has ever said to me. And the emotion filling her eyes is all the explanation I need. I know all about that emotion.

But she has to say it. Out loud.

"Why?" I ask.

"Because . . ." She closes her eyes and—I can see beneath the water—clutches Brody's hand. "I love him."

She means it. I don't know how I can know for certain, except that everything I see in her eyes is what I feel when I look at Quince.

"You know what this means?" I ask. Both of them.

"Yes," Doe says quickly. "I've explained everything. *Everything.*"

"And you're okay with this?" I ask Brody.

He gives Doe an equally emotional look. "I am."

"We've talked it out," Doe explains. "I'll stay on land until after graduation. Then we can spend the summer in Thalassinia. When Brody starts college, we'll go home on breaks and holidays."

"You're willing to give up your swimming?" This has to be the hardest part about Brody's decision. "You know chlorine will start to be toxic to you as soon as you turn."

"I do." His golden brown gaze doesn't waver from mine. "Doe says I'll be able to tolerate it long enough to swim at State."

I nod. None of the mer changes are instantaneous. Most are a gradual progression, so it's not likely that chlorine will kill him if he races in the next few weeks. "That's probably true."

"That's enough for me," he says. "Swimming is for now, Doe is forever."

My tears well again at the certainty in his voice. They really have talked this through.

And if Doe is willing to spend that much time on land to be with the boy she loves . . . well, then, she must be over her hate for humans, too. I guess this is the best possible outcome for everybody. Doe isn't going to try to wipe out the East Coast again. Brody gets to spend time in an underwater kingdom. And Doe has found her perfect mer mate.

But if things are so froggin' awesome, then why do I feel like bawling?

"Are you okay, Lil?" Brody asks.

"Is it so bad?" Doe asks, her voice full of tears. "Seeing me happy with the boy you used to love?"

"No," I sob.

"Used to love?" he asks, teasing me like the same old Brody as always. "Lil never really loved me."

"She thought she did," Doe says. And, as mortifying as that should be, I don't think she said it to be mean.

"But you're happy with Fletcher, right?" Brody asks. "You're not still—"

"I'm not," I interrupt. "I'm way over you. It's just that—" *Sniff, sob.* "I'm so happy for you."

Since I finished that on a wail, I'm not sure they exactly believe me. In an instant I'm wrapped in a group hug.

"What happened?" Doe asks. "Is this about Tellin's toast?"

I nod, incapable of speech. She's more insightful than I gave her credit for.

A long silence passes around me.

"Tell her," Brody says. "She needs to know."

The hug breaks up, and Doe turns me to face her. There's more of that newfound seriousness in her eyes.

"Lily, there's something you should know about Tellin." She swallows, as if sucking up her courage. "Over the past few years, he and I became friends."

Okay. Not completely out of the realm of possibility.

"When you made the decision to give up your crown, I went to him. I thought you were making a huge mistake, and that Thalassinia would pay the price for your selfish choice." She rolls her eyes as if she can't believe what she's about to say. "I thought we needed you as our queen."

"Really? You think so?" I ask, shocked by her confidence in me. Since she's never shown me anything other than contempt and disregard, I'm a little stunned by her confession. When she throws me a look, I quickly get back on track. "What does that have to do with Tellin?"

"He feels the same way," Doe continues. "That without you as heir to the throne, Thalassinia and all her sister kingdoms will suffer."

"I'm thrilled by your faith in me," I say, annoyed that she

seems to be swimming around the point, "but what does that have to do with anything?"

"We formed a plan," she says. "One that would force you to go home before your birthday. Where you could run into Tellin and he could make his proposal."

You know that sinking feeling I've been getting in my stomach a lot lately? I'm getting it again. Triple time.

"What kind of plan?"

"The tsunami and the bond with Brody." She closes her eyes, like she's afraid of my reaction. "They were a plot to put you back in Tellin's path."

"A what?" This doesn't make any sense. "Why? I don't understand."

"Lily," Doe says, sounding exasperated, "I got exiled *on purpose.*"

"On purpose?" I shake my head. "Why would you do that?"

"Partly because it gave me a taste of revenge on humans. But also so I could bond with some unsuspecting boy." She jerks her head at Brody. "So you would have to take him home for the separation."

"All of that," I ask, "just to force a chance run-in with Tellin?"

"I didn't say it was a brilliant plan," she says, blinking. "Besides, it worked, didn't it?"

Of all the stupid, idiotic, imprudent—see, I *have* learned my SAT vocabulary—ill-conceived plans in the history of the mer world, this has got to be in the top ten.

Still confused, I ask, "Why are you telling me this now?"

"Because I fell in love," she explains, floating up against Brody's side. "And because you're in love, too. Now I know what you'd be giving up to bond with Tellin." She seems to draw in on herself. "I would never wish that on you. I'm sorry."

I still don't think I fully understand. But this is a whole new Dosinia before me. One with the kind of maturity I'd always hoped to see in her.

If I weren't so angry about her irresponsible plotting and what it might have cost me—what it might *still* cost me—I would actually hug her for growing up. The waters might have been a little rough along the way, but what matters most is that she got there in the end. She apologized—can you say shock?—she accepted responsibility, and she's in love with a human. That's one part of my current dilemma solved.

Now if only Quince would come home so we could talk things out. Then life would be back to pretty darn near perfect.

14

*U*sually I love Sunday mornings—I sleep late and spend some lazy time in bed, Aunt Rachel makes a doughnut run, and Quince comes over to wipe the sprinkles off my cheek. But the moment I wake up, I feel like something is wrong. Quince still hasn't come home.

When I pad downstairs in my rainbow pajamas and find Aunt Rachel returning from grabbing the newspaper from the front yard—something Quince usually does for her— and an untouched white paper bag on the table, I know my feeling is confirmed. He isn't here.

"Janet says he called her last night," Aunt Rachel says, practically reading my thoughts. "He told her to tell you happy birthday for him."

I pull out one of the chairs at the kitchen table and half sink, half collapse onto the wooden seat. "He's not coming back."

"Doesn't look like it, sweetie," she says, taking the chair next to me and laying her hand over mine. "Not right away, anyway. He'll come home eventually."

I can't believe he is *this* angry about everything. I mean, I'm not asking him to give anything up or make any sacrifices, and the ones I'm making are *my* choices. No one forced me to love him and live on land. It's just the only thing that makes sense.

"I'm sure he needs some time to digest the situation," she suggests.

"I don't have time," I tell her. "I have to go home this afternoon for the final fitting of my dress and to go over the last-minute party details with Margarite. How can I leave like this? When he's not even speaking to me?"

"You will because you have to." She squeezes my hand. "You are the royal princess of Thalassinia, and you will do what needs to be done."

Yeah, I'm the princess. For two more days, anyway.

"Can you—" I begin. "If he comes back, will you—?"

Aunt Rachel must understand my mangled meaning, because she says, "When he comes home, I'll send you a messenger gull."

"Thank you."

Messenger gulls are usually used to send messages from the mer world to our kin on land, but there are always a few hanging out at every pier, just in case a land-based merperson needs to send a message home. Aunt Rachel knows how to call them.

At least I won't have to spend my time at home constantly worrying if Quince is back or not. Until I receive that message, I'll know he's still gone.

"I'm going to go finish the last of my homework," I say, pushing away from the table without a second glance at the bag of doughnuts. "Shannen's coming by later to pick it up. She's taking me to lunch before I head home."

Aunt Rachel just nods sadly.

I trudge back upstairs and open my trig textbook, only to stare blankly at the page of homework problems for the next few hours. Not even the warmth of Prithi's furry weight on my toes lifts my spirits. She's only returning her attentions to me because Doe locked her out.

I'm still zoned out over my unfinished homework when the phone rings. My heart pounds. I'm out of my chair, sending Prithi scurrying under my bed, and at my door in an instant, jerking so hard it bounces against the wall and back into my shoulder.

"I've got it!" I shout down the stairs as I dash across the hall to grab the call. I pant, "Hello?"

"Lily," a woman's voice says, "it's Miss Molina."

"Miss Mo—" I start to ask her why she's calling, but then I know. "Oh, no," I whisper. "Not again."

The interview. Which was supposed to be yesterday. The

one I'd totally forgotten in the middle of all my personal drama.

"I'm so sorry," I say, even though I know it's inadequate. "I really meant to go, right after the SATs, but things have been kind of crazy around here lately and I had this huge fight with my boyfriend, which isn't really an excuse, I know, but I was so preoccupied and—"

"Lily." Her serious tone stops my babble midbab. "I understand that you have a lot going on right now. Most students do."

I sense a big, giant-squid-sized but coming.

"But," she says, "I wonder if there is a reason you have missed both of your interview appointments."

"There is," I explain. "I really wanted to go—"

"Did you?"

"I—" What does she mean? "Of course I did."

"I know your decision to attend college is a recent one," she says. "Maybe, I don't know, maybe you still aren't certain."

"What do you mean?"

I hear her take a deep breath. "Maybe you don't really want to go to college. Maybe you're sabotaging your chances so the decision is made for you."

"That's ridiculous." She has no idea what's really going on, and it's not like I can explain it to her. "I do want to go to college. Really, I do."

"If this kind of irresponsible behavior is uncharacteristic, maybe your subconscious is trying to tell you something."

"It's not," I insist. "Really! I've just had a crazy week."

"I want you to think about it," she says, gently but firmly. "If you are still committed to the decision two weeks from now, I will see about arranging another interview."

"I don't need to think about it." I know I sound desperate, but this is like the final kelp strand that broke the sea horse's back. Just one thing too many swirling out of my control. "I swear, it's just—"

"Two weeks," she states. "I'll see you in school tomorrow."

"But—"

She's gone before I can tell her that I won't be in school tomorrow. Great—that will probably just reassure her that I don't really even want to be in school, let alone go to college.

I slam the phone back down on the base.

That's so unfair. She has no clue what's going on. How can she pretend to guess what my subconscious is thinking?

"Why does everything seem to be spiraling out of control?" I ask no one in particular.

I don't expect an answer.

"Anything I can help with?" a deep male voice asks.

"Daddy!"

I spin away from the phone, shocked to see him standing in the upstairs hall. In a fin flick I'm in his arms, squealing, "What are you doing here?"

229

"Can't a father visit his daughter?"

"He can," I say, pulling back to give him a fake-stern look, "but he usually doesn't. Not when his calendar is full of kingly duties and his daughter lives on land."

"Well, it's a special week," he explains. "It's not every day my only child turns eighteen."

"But I'm coming home tonight," I explain. "You would have seen me in a few hours anyway."

Not that I'm not thrilled to see him.

He gets a mischievous look in his eyes. "What I have to do cannot be done under water."

He looks totally pleased with himself, like he's got the greatest secret in the history of merkind. At times like this he seems more like a little boy than the most powerful man in Thalassinia.

"What?" I ask warily.

He gestures for me to take a seat on my bed, which I do because I want to find out his secret.

"For the past few weeks I have had Mangrove scouring the royal records for something." He sits next to me on the bed. "For something I remember my father alluding to but I wasn't sure existed or was even possible."

"What?" The anticipation is killing me.

"You know that every merperson is branded with the mer mark on his or her neck."

"Of course." I roll my eyes. "Daddy . . ."

"What you may not know is that the mark is not only a

symbol," he explains, "but also the source of our powers."

I think back to the image of Doe's incomplete mer mark. That makes sense. When he exiled her and revoked her powers, the outer circle of her mer mark disappeared. When he lifts the exile, it will probably return.

"What Mangrove found," Daddy says, sounding like he might be actually getting to the point, "is an ancient ritual for creating the mark."

"Creating the mark?" I echo. "What does that mean?"

"Merfolk did not always exist," he explains. "We were human until Capheira used Poseidon's trident to grants us *aqua vide*."

"This isn't news," I insist. "It's ancient history. What does it have to do with today?"

"What this means, Lily," he says, his face melting into one of pure joy, "is that I can use that ritual to bestow the powers of our people on a human."

I gasp. And tears tingle at the inner corners of my eyes. He doesn't have to finish the thought, because I immediately know exactly what he means.

"I can grant Quince the power of aquarespire," he finishes, "even without the bond. Your young man can come home with you."

My emotions erupt in a battle between joy—Quince can return to Thalassinia!—and despair. Quince is gone. After all the ups and downs and whirlarounds of the last few weeks, it's no wonder I have kind of a mini meltdown. I break into great gasping sobs.

Not, I imagine, the reaction Daddy had been hoping for.

"What's wrong?" He wraps a strong arm around my shoulders and hugs me close. "What happened?"

"Quince left," I blurt between sobs. "He found out I'm giving up the crown to be with him," I explain, "and he left."

"Where did he go?"

Shaking my head, I answer, "I don't know. He was just so angry." I wipe at my nose. "He doesn't think he's worth the sacrifice."

There is a tense pause before Daddy says, "But you do?"

"Of course!" How can he even ask me that? "He's the kindest, strongest, most loyal person I've ever known. I *love* him."

Daddy nods, as if pleased by my answer. "Then everything will work out."

I suck in a deep breath and glance at the ceiling. "I'm not sure."

"It will just take time," Daddy says, patting my knee.

"I know." I wipe at the tears, trying to regain some composure. "Hopefully he'll be home by the time I get back. We can talk then."

"Do you want to postpone the ball?" he asks. "We cannot delay the renunciation, but we could reschedule the party."

"No," I insist. "No, I'll be fine." Ish. I climb off the bed. "Let's get going now. I'm sure Peri and her mom are eager to finish my gown."

232

"Are you certain?" His eyes are full of concern. "We could wait; maybe Quince will return in time to—"

"I'm sure." The last thing I want is to have it out with my boyfriend while my dad is waiting. What Quince and I have to talk about won't change in the next few days—even though my decision will have been made final.

"Just let me call Shannen to cancel lunch," I say, "and tell Aunt Rachel and Doe good-bye."

"How is your cousin doing, by the way?" Daddy asks. "Have you made any progress with her?"

I freeze halfway to the door. Shoot, this wasn't how I'd imagined telling him Doe's news.

"Actually . . ."

"Lily cured me," Doe says, appearing in my open doorway and saving me from explaining. She spoons a bite of key lime yogurt into her mouth.

"Did she?" Daddy asks.

"I'm bonded to Brody," Doe says with a little sass. As if expecting an argument, and totally ready for it. She licks her spoon. "Permanently. I love him."

I think Doe and I are both shocked at Daddy's response.

"Huh," he says, pulling his mouth into a considering look. "Interesting."

That's it? Interesting?

Maybe Daddy's losing it in his old age.

"Lily, why don't you go make your phone call," he says, not taking his eyes off Doe. "I'll be down in a moment."

Maybe he's not losing it. He just doesn't want to scold her in front of me. Sorry, Doe. She hands me her empty yogurt container and spoon as I pass by, and I lose a little of my sympathy.

"Okay," I say, hurrying into the hall before the yelling match begins. I just hope I don't get any of the leftover wrath for not performing the separation ritual as agreed.

Twenty minutes later, Aunt Rachel is waving good-bye to us at Seaview Beach, and Daddy and I are heading into the waves. Despite all the looming craziness—my ball gown, the party details, the party, the title renunciation ritual— all I can think about is the hope that Quince will be home when I get back.

My first birthday wish is coming true. Now I know what wish I'll be making over my underwater birthday cake.

15

"You look . . ." I sense Peri moving away from me. "Breathtaking. Open your eyes."

When they performed the final fitting on Sunday night, Peri and her mom kept me blindfolded so I couldn't see what the dress looked like. Now, less than an hour before my party, Peri has dressed me with my eyes closed.

The anticipation is killing me.

My first sight of the dress—of me in the dress—nearly knocks my breath away. Though I knew vaguely what the dress would look like from the pattern mock-up they pinned to me last week, the final product is so far beyond anything I could have imagined that I am completely stunned.

The halter top has a deep plunging V that, while reaching almost to my navel, manages to be completely modest. From the waist, the skirt hugs the curves of my tail fin to the knee joint, before flaring out into a reverse-V hem. Dozens of ruffled layers fluff out the skirt in a million shades of green with subtle hints of gold.

I recognize the petticoat fabric. It's the cloth Peri was working on when I came home last week.

In the back, the hem trails off into a point several feet longer than my fin. The tail waves gently back and forth behind me in the soft current of the Gulf Stream.

And the best part? The body of the dress is a magical shade of gold. At this moment it perfectly matches the tear-glittered shade of my eyes.

"Thank you," I whisper. "The dress is amazing."

"Mom and I knew we needed something extra special," Peri explains, "for your last gown as a royal princess."

If my eyes hadn't already been glittering with tears, they would be now. Not because I'm sad, but because my life is about to change. Permanently. In a few short hours I will no longer be Princess Waterlily. I'll be plain old Lily Sanderson, insignificant daughter of the king.

It's a choice I've happily made, but that doesn't mean the change is easy to accept.

"Come on," Peri says, fussing with the green ruffles of my hem, "let's get down to that party. I've heard the birthday girl is a total diva."

We're still giggling as we swim up to the private entrance to the royal ballroom. Mangrove, Daddy's trusted secretary, is guarding the door. Ready to announce my arrival.

236

"You look beautiful, Princess," he says, bending low over his fin.

"Thank you, Mangrove," I reply dutifully.

His hand on the door, he asks, "Shall I announce your arrival?"

After a quick shared look with Peri, I nod.

He pulls the door open wide, swims into the room, and using his most ceremonial voice, bellows, "Princess Waterlily."

A hush falls across the ballroom.

I force myself not to think about the last time I entered the royal ballroom on a wave of silent anticipation—Quince-related memories will only make me cry more at this point.

Instead, I focus on the crowd, on hundreds of merfolk dressed in their finest apparel, and on the ballroom. The ceiling covered in gold and green seaweed streamers, six different buffet tables of the most mouthwatering delicacies in the ocean, a school of lightning-bug fish—a uniquely Thalassinian species—swimming amid the streamers, making the ceiling twinkle with their flashing lights. It's every mergirl's dream. The only thing that could have made it more perfect would be if—

No, I can't think about him right now. For the next few hours I need to be Princess Waterlily, not Princess Waterpot. I want my last moments as a royal princess to be proud ones. They'll have to last me a lifetime.

"Happy birthday, daughter," Daddy says, sweeping me into a massive hug and—thankfully—saving me from a Quince-related thought.

"Thank you, Daddy," I say, hugging him back. "It's beautiful."

A mergirl's eighteenth birthday is supposed to be the most magical day of her life. She is officially an adult, as far as the mer world is concerned, and all of her family and friends join in the celebration.

A *royal* mergirl's eighteenth birthday is even more special. There is a huge buffet feast, which makes the one at Dosinia's sixteenth birthday look like an after-school snack. In the far corner of the room, an eighteen-piece orchestra is playing a program of fun-yet-classical compositions. Women in gem- and pearl-encrusted gowns dance with men in sharp tuxedo jackets with gem- and pearl-encrusted cummerbunds. It's like a fantasy world. Everything around me is glittery and sparkly and full of laughter and fun.

Everything except me.

If I were a bonded princess, this is the day I would go from royal to crowned. Accepting my future role as queen. When I made the decision to stay on land a few weeks ago, I knew exactly what I was getting into. I knew what I would be giving up, that I would be letting my kingdom and my ancestors down. I knew it, and I didn't care. With so many of the things I care about most tied to land, I would make a miserable queen. And a miserable

238

queen can hardly be a good leader.

Still, despite all my thinking and rationalizing and accepting, I didn't know it would be this hard, that my feelings would be this painful, when the moment came.

Instead of sparkling gowns and formal jackets, I see my future subjects. These are the people, along with the thousands beyond the palace walls, I'll be leaving heirless. Are my selfish wants worth what it will cost *them*?

"Good evening, Princess Waterlily."

I turn and find a trio of girls my age bowing into the water. They look like coordinating Oceanista dolls. One has pale skin, red hair, and a mint green tail fin. One has a fake tan, bright blond hair, and an orange-gold tail fin. And one has naturally dark skin, long flowing black curls, and a glinting mahogany tail fin.

The terrible trio. Though I haven't seen them in years, I recognize them from my early tutoring sessions in the palace.

As I said, they never seemed to like me very much.

"Hello, Astria," I say to the redhead, the leader; then to the other two, "Piper, Venus."

Piper's eyes widen. Probably surprised that I remembered their names after all these years.

"We are honored to be a part of your birthday celebration, Princess," Astria says, all mocking respect.

I could tell her to call me Lily, but since I'm pretty sure that's what she wants, I don't. The tiny hairs on the back of my neck are at attention, and I have a feeling this is going to end badly.

This is my last birthday as the royal princess of Thalassinia, and I'm not about to let three snobby clones ruin it for me.

"Of course," I reply magnanimously, bowing my head slightly. "Now, if you'll excuse me—"

"It's too bad," Astria interrupts.

I freeze in my escape.

"Really," Venus agrees. "Too, too bad."

"Too, too bad," Piper parrots.

"If only . . . ," Astria says.

She leaves it hanging, like a grub on a hook, waiting for me to bite. I shouldn't. I know I shouldn't. Astria, Piper, and Venus have been trouble since we were guppies. They're the reason Daddy made me spend a week scraping the algae off the palace roof when I was nine, for something that wasn't even my fault.

Still, knowing all that, I can't help but ask, "If only what?"

Astria gives me an appallingly sympathetic look. "If only you had found a boy willing to bond with you."

"Such a shame," Venus commiserates.

My mouth drops open. They have *no* idea. I'm on the verge of setting them straight when I feel a warm arm wrap around my waist.

"Has Lily been telling you how she rebuffed my advances?" Tellin asks, hugging me close to his side. "I've been begging her to bond with me for ages, but she just won't relent." He smiles at me. "Loves her human too much."

My three tormentors suck in identical gasps. Since he's dressed in Acropora's finest royal uniform, they know exactly who he is. And *what* he is.

Take that, sea witches.

They are still slack-jawed when Tellin says, "I believe this is my dance."

As he tugs me away, I glance back over my shoulder. The look of utter shock on their faces is the best moment of the night.

Even though I'm still mad at him for the whole Quince-revelation thing and the whole conspiring-with-Doe thing, the saving-me-from-the-terrible-trio thing is enough to cool my anger a little.

"Thanks," I say as he leads me into an open spot of the dance area in front of the orchestra. "Those three almost put Dosinia to shame."

"You are quite welcome," Tellin says, pulling me into his arms for the dance.

Now that we're out of range of the terrible trio, I refocus on why I'm mad at him. Social savior or not, he has a lot to answer for.

"Doe told me about your plan."

He doesn't miss a beat in the music. "Did she?"

"She did, and—" I'm not sure how to say exactly what I think of that, so I blurt, "I appreciate your faith in my abilities as a leader, but it was all kinds of ridiculous from the start, wasn't it?"

"Perhaps," he says with a gentle smile. Then, changing the subject, he says, "I must confess my motives for rescuing you from those girls were not entirely selfless."

"What do you mean?" I ask, even though I'm pretty sure I already know.

"I mean," he says, whirling me into a spin, "that I wanted the opportunity to plead my case one last time."

I wish he wouldn't. Not now. Not when I'm already plagued by doubts and guilt and stressed out about the situation with Quince and my chances of ever going to college. It would be almost too easy for him to succeed.

"You are what Thalassinia needs," he says. "Look at the merfolk around us. Spoiled, privileged, and without direction. They have no idea what strife and hardship are. They need *you* to guide them into the future."

As Tellin turns us in a slow circle, I say, "Not me."

I think about those times when I sat with Daddy in the throne room, listening to him preside over cases with the authority and magnanimity—woo-hoo, another SAT word usage in real life—that makes him the very best sort of ruler. I could never be as great as him.

"I'm not queen material."

"Do you think I am king material?" he asks with surprising sharpness. "I was not prepared to lead my kingdom, but when my father fell ill, I did not turn away from my duty."

242

I don't miss the subtle accusation. That I *am* turning away from my duty.

I force myself to ignore the jab.

Tellin looks every bit the king right now. There is nothing left of the young boy I used to play what if with.

"How did you do it?" I ask quietly.

"How? I didn't stop to think about how," he says. "I just did it. Because it had to be done."

"I—" I close my eyes. "I don't have the strength to be the queen. I'm not . . . I will never be enough."

"Lily," he says, pulling me close, "there is no such thing as a perfect ruler. Every king or queen has a weakness. The key is recognizing yours and compensating with your strengths."

"What strengths?" I ask. "What do I have to offer my kingdom?"

"Your compassion," he says instantly. "Your kindness, your heart, your loyalty, your unique experience."

My experience. On land, he means.

He's playing to all my doubts, tugging at my guilt. Could I be queen? Well, I know I *could* be queen, but could I be a *good* queen? Am I what my kingdom needs? Daddy has always been opposed to coming out of the ocean, certain that humankind is rarely the most tolerant and understanding of anything different or other. But what if he's wrong? Should I take up the mantle of my title and use my influence to pull the mer world out of the water?

My head is overflowing with thoughts. Too many things.

"I'm sorry," I say, pushing out of his arms. "I need to— I'm sorry."

I leave Tellin on the dance floor, floating in the middle of the swirling and whirling couples. I flee the room, slipping out the back entrance and winding my way through the service halls to the one place where I've always felt safest. Daddy's office.

With everyone, including the palace staff, at the party downstairs, I'm not surprised to find the royal wing deserted. Daddy's office is empty and dark. As soon as I swim through the door, the bioluminescent light in the ceiling comes to life, filling the room with a soft blue glow.

I absently drift to the right, to the wall of mosaic portraits depicting my ancestors. The many before me who ruled Thalassinia with varying degrees of effectiveness. They weren't all perfect, I know, but they were better than me.

First on the wall is Daddy, our latest king. His portrait depicts him seated at his desk, the trident in his right hand and a clump of chenille weed in his left, representing strength and integrity. He looks so young. He took the throne when he was not much older than Tellin, I suppose. Maybe Daddy was just as uncertain, and just as determined to do his best.

Next on the wall is my grandfather. He passed long before I was born, so I have no memories of him beyond this portrait. He is standing on the balcony of the royal chamber, presumably looking out over his subjects gathered below. The people called him Pecten the Generous because he was quite free with the kingdom's funds. Which is also why Daddy had to spend the first part of his reign restoring the treasury.

Before grandfather, there was Teredo the Just, the Golden Queen Alaria, Marianus the Cautious, and Quahog the Magnificent. He's the one who got eaten by a giant squid because his guards couldn't get down the royal aisle—aka the Bimini Road—fast enough. Not so much common sense. Guess they meant magnificent in other ways. A dozen more faces grace the walls, ancestors whose names I barely remember but whose blood—and duty—runs in my veins.

Such a legacy.

Am I crazy to give this up?

"Your portrait should be next."

My entire body sighs.

"I didn't ask you to follow me, Tellin."

"I know," he says, swimming up next to me.

I'm staring at the last portrait—which was the first one created. My great-many-times-over grandfather, Chiton, the first king of Thalassinia. The one whom Capheira, our mythological ancestor, first granted the gift of mer life. He doesn't look that different from Daddy, a similar face with white hair and a short white beard. Same smiling blue eyes.

"Lily, you can't just let this slip away," he pleads. "There

245

is too much riding on your future."

"Thalassinia will find another heir," I reply, turning to face him.

"But when?" he demands. "And what sort? You've trained for this your entire life. You've been bred for this."

He braces his arms against the wall on either side of my shoulders.

"Tellin, I—"

I interrupt my own thought. Here in the utter privacy of Daddy's office, with the dim lights and in the cage of Tellin's arms, it almost feels . . . right. He's so close and so passionate about making choices for the common good. My duty, my responsibility. My destiny. It's only a kiss away.

It would be so easy just to lean forward a few inches, press my lips to his, and vanquish all my doubts and guilt forever. So easy . . .

An image of Quince flashes in my mind.

I can't.

Just because something is the easy choice does not make it the right one. Quite often the right choice is really, really hard. I've made my decision. I love Quince and I believe my future lies on land. I'm not about to throw all of that away to avoid snide comments from girls like Astria or to wash away guilt that Daddy has assured me I don't need to feel.

"Tellin," I say, pressing a palm to his chest to push him away, "I can't. I have to make my own choices in life, or it won't be my life."

"Damn it!" Tellin slams a palm against the wall so hard I feel the vibrations—quite a feat under water. "Lily, you can't do this. You're going to ruin everything."

"What?" I have never seen that kind of fury in his pale eyes. "Ruin what?"

"You have no idea," he says, his voice a rough growl. "My kingdom . . ." A look of complete desperation washes over his face. "We're dying, Lily. With the rising ocean temperatures, the coral in our kingdom can't survive. It's disrupting the entire cycle of life in our waters."

I suck in a gasp. I knew that ocean warming was a worldwide problem, that the mer kingdoms had been in talks for years about how to combat the effects. But I didn't know any kingdoms had been so dramatically affected already.

Thalassinia has been lucky in its more northerly location. We've seen new species migrating into our waters, but so far that's only been an interesting sea forestry study. Down in the already warm waters of the Caribbean, in an ecosystem so entirely dependent on the coral reefs, I can't imagine what Acropora must be going through.

"I'm so sorry," I say, even though I know it's totally inadequate.

"Sorry," he scoffs. "Lily, my father isn't ill, he's dying. My people are starving. I haven't been living on land because I want to. I've *had* to. Many of my subjects have been forced to either leave the waters or emigrate to other kingdoms."

"That's awful," I say, cupping his cheek in sympathy. "But

I don't see how bonding with me——"

"You don't see?" he spits. "Uniting our kingdoms is the only hope. With the strength and prosperity of Thalassinia comes the salvation my people need."

"But——" I shake my head. "Our bonding would not unite the kingdoms. You said it would be a bond in name only, so I could take the throne."

"You are either very naive or willfully blind," he snorts. "And selfish."

I have no response to that because, well, *am* I being selfish? I can't tell anymore.

"You have doubts," he pleads. "I can see you do." He floats down and lays his head against my belly. "For the love of your merkin to the south, I am begging you."

This is so much to take in. The fact that he's been lying to me about the bond. The famine and ecological destruction wiping out his kingdom. So much emotion. It's a lot to process, and the only thing I know is I am not the solution. I can't be. Right?

Thalassinia is a prosperous and wealthy kingdom, and we are very generous with those less fortunate, but we don't have the capability to support an entire second kingdom. Especially one as large and diverse as Acropora.

Tellin's hopes for a united kingdom are unrealistic.

"Tellin, I'm very sorry for your kingdom's suffering," I say, feeling helpless. I gently wrap my arms around his shoulders. "But bonding with me won't——"

"The hell it won't," he growls before suddenly kicking upward until his face is level with mine. "It's the only option we have."

His abrupt movements are such a surprise, his lips are nearly on mine before I react. I twist to the side, dislodging his body, and—with a flick of my fin—I'm out of his arms and in the center of the room.

He doesn't chase after me. He just drops his head against the wall. His shoulders are heaving and I think he might be crying. Sobbing.

"Tellin . . ." I swim back toward him, overcome by sympathy. Maybe I should be angry, but desperation makes people do uncharacteristic things.

"Don't. That was unforgivable." He shrugs off my hand on his shoulder. "I'm sorry, Lily. I am so sorry."

I take a deep breath. This is my friend speaking, not the desperate king of moments ago.

"I understand," I say, floating to his side. "You are worried about your kingdom."

He looks at me, his pale eyes bleak and lost. And glittering ice blue. "I'm worried that, if things don't change, there won't be a kingdom much longer."

So much pressure on one so young. No wonder he tried to take such drastic action. To find out that your father is dying and your kingdom might be, too? That's a lot to deal with.

He shouldn't have to deal with it alone.

"Have you spoken to Daddy?" I ask. "Or to the other kings and queens?"

The mer kingdoms are all unique and sovereign nations, but we are joined by a common secrecy, a common heritage. We try to protect and help one another out as much as we can.

"My father wouldn't let me," he says. "Too proud to ask for help."

I know that pride is a powerful emotion, but it is also a terrible indulgence. Especially when the fate of your kingdom is at stake.

"Your father is not in charge at the moment." I take Tellin's hand in mine, showing my support. "You can move beyond his pride."

"You know," he says with a sad laugh, "that's why he stopped speaking with your father. Because King Whelk refused to sign the arranged bond agreement for us. My father can't stand the thought of being denied."

Well, at least that makes more sense. I couldn't really see Daddy wanting to arrange a marriage for me, not since he's been so adamant that I follow my heart.

I shake off my annoyance at Tellin's father. "You need to call a council of kings and queens," I suggest. "Present them with your situation, and I'm sure you will not walk away without numerous promises of assistance."

"You are too generous," he says, squeezing my hand. "Fletcher is a lucky man."

"I like to think so," a new male voice says.

I spin around so fast, Tellin is pulled in my wake.

"Quince!" I squeal. Then I'm across the room, throwing my arms around his neck and peppering his face with kisses.

"Such a shame," Doe says, drifting in after Quince. "I was hoping to ruin your party like you ruined mine." She sighs. "Looks like I brought the guest of honor instead."

Ignoring Doe, I scream, "You're here!" I squeeze him tight. "What are you doing here?" Then I suddenly realize just exactly where *here* is, and I say, "*How* are you here?"

With a smile, Quince pulls my arms from around him and twists—awkwardly, because he's still in human form and still not the best swimmer—and shows me his neck. There is a black circle of waves tattooed at the base. The outer portion of the mer mark.

I am completely overcome with joyful, tearful emotion.

"Daddy found you?" I manage.

"Actually," Daddy says, swimming up next to Doe, "your cousin found him. I merely performed the ceremony when she brought him to me."

I glance, teary eyed, at everyone in the room. My squid-brained cousin, who's turning out to be not such a horrible young mermaid. My darling daddy, who found a way to bring me and Quince even closer together. My adored Quince, who is willing to accept all the craziness that comes along with life with me.

"We have something to talk about," I tell him, trying to

sound stern but knowing that my glittering eyes and huge smile undermine the effect.

"I know," he says with a matching smile. "I acted like an ass."

"Well . . ." That takes a lot of the steam out of my lecture. "Okay. As long as you recognize the fact."

He flashes me a wink. "Always."

"You know, daughter," Daddy says, swimming over his desk and sinking into the massive chair behind it, "it is nearly midnight."

Oh, no.

My heart starts beating flipper fast. I've been anticipating this moment for weeks now—sometimes eagerly, sometimes less so. But I've known it was coming. Now that it's here, I'm a little (a lot) freaked out.

"Mangrove and I have drawn up the papers." He pulls a few sheets of kelpaper from a drawer and sets them on top of the desk. "They only require your signature."

I swim up to the desk, painfully aware that all eyes in the room are on me. Daddy hands me a pen. I didn't expect it to happen this fast.

"Right here." He points to the line where I'm supposed to sign. Where, with one curl of ink on paper, I'll renounce my claim to the throne. Forever.

This is what I want, I remind myself. To be on land, with Quince and Aunt Rachel and lip gloss and mediocre sushi.

The squid ink–filled quill clutched in my fingers, I move

252

my hand over the paper. Over the line.

Hovering.

My entire body freezes, like Peri when a jellyfish floats by. I can't move a muscle. My brain is racing. Is this the right decision? Easy or hard, is this the best choice for my future, for the future of Thalassinia and of Acropora and the other mer kingdoms?

I have never felt so completely paralyzed by doubt.

Eyes wide, I seek out Quince, my rock. He's floating between Doe and Tellin, watching me calmly, betraying no emotion. When my gaze flicks to Tellin and back to Quince, his look shifts. Like he's bracing himself.

Then, in a moment that's just between us, Quince nods.

I don't need to voice the question I know he's answering. Our connection is stronger than any formed by a magical bond. And always will be.

Without giving myself time to think about the situation, I drop the pen, jet myself across the room with one power-ful kick, and grab Tellin by the shoulders. I only have an instant to register the pure shock in his eyes before my lips brush his.

16

*H*oly bananafish, what did I do? My brain freaks out for a second—okay, more than a second—not quite believing what my heart just told me to do.

But my brain quickly catches on. This is about more than love and college plans and a black-and-white decision between living on land or becoming queen. There is a huge, Pacific-sized gray area where I can choose both.

And I just did.

Holy bananafish!

The shock of my spontaneous decision sends gallons of adrenaline pouring into my bloodstream. While I take a few deep, calming breaths to regain a normal pulse, I take note of the room around me. The people around me.

Tellin blinks, like, forty-seven times.

Daddy shouts, "What have you done?"

Doe shrugs and stares at the ceiling with a bored expression.

Quince watches me seriously, silently, with his mouth drawn up into a smile on one side. He's not thrilled with the kiss, of course, but he supports my decision. I can tell. And it's a huge relief.

Since Daddy is the only one actively questioning my actions, I say, "It's the right thing to do." I share a solemn look with Tellin. "In more ways than one."

"Are you sure this is what you want?" Daddy asks after the two minutes it takes him to get over his shock. "There is still time to perform a separation, if you—"

"No." Though my decision was rash and instantaneous, I'm not racked by any feelings of regret. Actually, I'm relieved. The doubts that have been plaguing me for the last few weeks are instantly gone, telling me I made the right choice. "I am Thalassinia's princess, and I cannot cast aside that responsibility for selfish reasons."

Daddy's gaze shifts to Quince. "And you have no objections?"

"Sir," Quince says, floating to my side, "I am still a stranger to this world"—he takes my hand—"but I know your daughter. I believe she will be the best possible kind of ruler. I love her and will always support her choices in any way I can."

Daddy nods at Tellin. "And the bond?"

Quince squeezes my hand. "Our love is stronger than a bond," he says with the kind of certainty I've come to rely on. "If this is what it takes for Lily to remain in line for the crown, then this is what we have to do."

I squeeze his hand back. The best part of what he said? *We.* We are in this together, like the inscription on his birthday gift, forever. Who could ask for a better boyfriend?

Although this does mean I'll probably be hearing a super-sized I-told-you-so about the giving-up-my-crown bit. I'm okay with that.

"Guys, I know this is a lot to take in," I say. "But I need a minute alone with Tellin."

Daddy shakes his head, as if he still thinks I'm a little insane. He's probably right, but that doesn't mean I made the wrong choice. In time he'll see it's the only decision I could make.

"I'm going to enjoy the party before all the candy-coated sand strawberries are gone," Doe announces, continuing her bored attitude.

"Dosinia," I say before she disappears out the door. When she looks back over her shoulder, I say, "Thank you. For finding Quince. And other things."

I can't come out and thank her for the earthquake and the plot with Tellin, but we both know that she had a lot to do with my final decision.

She shrugs. "Whatever."

I catch sight of her smile before she swims out into the hall.

"I'll see you downstairs?" Quince asks.

I give him a solid kiss—just in case he or anyone else in the room has lingering doubts about my decision. "Wait right outside."

He nods at Tellin before following Daddy and Doe out the door.

"Lily, I—" Tellin begins.

"Don't." I turn on him. "Don't thank me or apologize or whatever else you were about to say. I didn't do this for you. I did it because it was the right thing to do. Because the oceans are changing and I want to help my kingdom and yours—and all the others—make the transition."

I thought I could be content to fight for the oceans from above, but things are more dire than I'd imagined. We're going to have to be more aggressive, more diligent. If I can help from land *and* from the throne room, then the chances I can help will definitely multiply.

He grins like the little merboy who used to dare me to eat sea slugs.

"You are every inch the future queen I knew you could be."

"Don't think you can butter me up," I say, waving his compliment away. "This is a political arrangement only. My heart belongs to Quince."

"I understand."

"And we'll scour the records to see if there is a way to remove the emotional connection from the bond." Not that I'm super worried about that, because I believe Quince's assertion that our love is stronger than the bond. But just in case . . . Besides, if Daddy can find a ritual to return Quince to the sea, then who knows what other rituals might be hiding in the archives? "We'll talk to Calliope Ebbsworth, our mer couples counselor, to see if she has any advice."

"Agreed." His smile turns sly. "My Lucina will be much relieved."

"Your Lucina?" I smack him on the shoulder. Is he joking? "Are you telling me you have a girlfriend?"

He has the decency to blush, a bright flaming pink beneath his cinnamon hair. "Yes."

"And she knew about your plan?"

"She is a mermaid of noble integrity," he says, his pale eyes glowing. "She understands the situation in our kingdom and why this connection is necessary."

I'm pretty sure I will never understand boys. Why is the truth so scary? He could have told me all of this days ago. Okay, so it probably wouldn't have affected my decision— which turned out to be in his favor anyway. I guess he won't be learning that lesson anytime soon.

"Come on," I say, swimming for the door. "We've got a party to attend."

Tellin swims after me. "And a trio of old acquaintances

with whom to share your news?"

My mood brightens by about a million percent. I hadn't thought of that. Astria is totally going to have to eat her words. Seeing the jealousy in her and her look-alikes' eyes will be so gratifying.

"Maybe I could play up my enthusiasm," I say, swimming up to Quince and slipping my arm around his. "Just a bit."

"Not too much," Quince says. "A guy needs to protect his image."

Tellin laughs, grabbing Quince's other arm. Though often masked by duty and responsibility, Tellin is still very much the merboy I remember. As we swim down to the ballroom, I can imagine far worse things than ruling with these two at my side.

"Ladies and gentlemen," Mangrove announces with the biggest smile I have ever seen on his face, "*Crown* Princess Waterlily of Thalassinia, Crown Prince Tellin of Acropora, and Master Quince Fletcher."

This time, the room erupts in whispers, as the realization that I am still Thalassinia's princess makes its way through the crowd. Far preferable to a stunned silence.

Quince, Tellin, and I swim through the doors, three abreast. I am in the middle, holding Quince's hand, our fingers laced tightly together. The message will be clear. Tellin and I are allies, not mermates.

"Subjects of Thalassinia," Daddy says, raising a glass of

sparkling gelatin—the mer equivalent of champagne—as the waitstaff scurries through the crowd with trays of the stuff. "Please raise your glasses in toast to my daughter. Thalassinia's future queen."

"Long live Princess Waterlily" echoes throughout the room as everyone in attendance lifts a glass in my honor.

It's a little overwhelming, the thought that sometime in the (hopefully very) distant future, I will be responsible for leading all the merfolk in this room and beyond. No, it's not overwhelming. It's terrifying.

Tellin grabs a pair of glasses from a passing waitress and hands them to me and Quince. At the same time, Mangrove appears with another pair.

"I'll take those," Doe says, grabbing the glasses from Mangrove and handing one to Tellin.

Mangrove looks like he wants to throttle her—welcome to my world—but then turns and swims quietly away.

"To Lily," Quince says, raising his glass.

Doe and Tellin echo, "To Lily."

I barely hear them. All I can focus on is the look of pride in Quince's eyes as he looks at me.

Can a mergirl get any luckier? I have the boy I love—and he has been restored to aquarespire—*and* my future as queen of Thalassinia. Of course there will be details to work out. Where we will live and when? Do I still want to go to college? What about Quince's plans for the future? How can I—and Thalassinia and the other kingdoms—help Tellin and the people of Acropora?

Sure, those are a lot of questions. But the best part is there's no longer a ticking clock. No eighteenth birthday looming over me like a time bomb.

We have time to figure it all out.

Together.

In the meantime, there are three girls who I am sure are just dying for an introduction to my boyfriend. Ever the dutiful public servant, I grab him by the wrist and head off for a little show-and-tell.

It's good to be the princess.